Margaret L Lee

Narcissus

Margaret L Lee

Narcissus

ISBN/EAN: 9783337398729

Printed in Europe, USA, Canada, Australia, Japan

Cover: Foto ©Andreas Hilbeck / pixelio.de

More available books at **www.hansebooks.com**

NARCISSUS

A TWELFE NIGHT MERRIMENT

PLAYED BY YOUTHS OF THE PARISH

AT

THE COLLEGE OF S. JOHN THE BAPTIST
IN OXFORD, A.D. 1602

WITH APPENDIX

NOW FIRST EDITED FROM A BODLEIAN MS.

BY

MARGARET L. LEE

OF S. HUGH'S HALL, OXFORD

LONDON

PUBLISHED BY DAVID NUTT IN THE STRAND

MDCCCXCIII

INTERLOQUUTORES.

1. TYRESIAS.
2. CEPHISUS.
3. NARCISSUS.
4. DORASTUS.
5. CLINIAS.

6. ECCHO.
7. LYRIOPE.
8. FLORIDA.
9. CLOIS.
10. THE WELL.

11. PORTER.

PREFACE.

N editing the hitherto unpublished play of *Narcissus*, together with the three speeches and the letter composed for Francis Clarke, porter of S. John's, I have retained throughout the very irregular spelling of the MS. The punctuation and use of capital letters have, however, been modernized, the contractions employed for *the*, *which*, *with*, *what*, and certain prefixes, expanded, and a few obviously scribal errors corrected in the text, the notes supplying in every such case the original MS. reading.

In bringing to its conclusion a work which now seems even less satisfactorily performed than I once hoped it might be, there is at least a pleasure in recording thanks to all those who have interested themselves on my behalf, and aided me with suggestions and criticisms, or—as in the case of the editors of the *N. E. D.*—with valuable references. Indeed, were it not for the direct and indirect help of friends—and amongst those who have given me the former I must make special and grateful mention of Professor Ker, Professor Napier, and Mr. Madan — *Narcissus* would have been left to find a worthier editor.

26, WARRINGTON CRESCENT,
    MAIDA HILL.

INTRODUCTION.

HIS play, which for want of a ready-made title I have called *Narcissus,* dates from a period of peculiar interest in the history of that class of dramatic composition to which it belongs.

So vast a phenomenon as the rise and fall of the complete English drama could not but be attended by widely-spread symptoms of the popular love for stage representation; a tendency which, though it would never have produced a Shaksperian tragedy, yet alone rendered possible the work of a Shakspere. These lesser manifestations of the feeling that pervaded Elizabethan England may be compared to the small fissures on the side of a volcano, through which the same lava as fills the molten crater emanates in slender and perhaps hardly perceptible channels. It may chance that the activity of these side-streams presages the final eruption at the summit; yet afterwards they are scarcely noticed, and their effects are too puny to attract attention. So it is with the abortive forms of drama, heralding, accompanying, and in some cases outliving, the culmination of English dramatic art under Shakspere. They are not, as a rule, the product of those great intel-lects which helped in the rearing of the main structure; but rather of such lesser writers as were either possessed by the dramatic spirit while ignorant of the formative and restraining rules of art, or else imbued with a desire to follow those rules, as they had been drawn up by Aristotle and Horace and exemplified in French and Italian literature, whilst themselves wanting in originality, and oblivious of the superiority of a native growth over the best of importations. The latter class of would-be English dramatists, in especial, found a natural field for action amongst the scholarly societies which constituted a mediæval university. Though as early as 1584 and 1593 statutes are found enacting that no players shall perform within five miles of Oxford, it must be remembered that these refer to professional, not to academical actors, and that the regulations controlling the former were of much greater stringency than those which concerned the latter.

Nor were plays imitated from Greek and Latin writers the only ones to be performed by undergraduates and others before select audiences in the college halls. Youthful players would probably demand the introduction of something more or less witty ; and the fact that theatrical representations generally took place on the occasion of a royal visit, or at times of special rejoicing, accounts in some degree for the casting .aside of the strictly classical models, and the employment of masques, or of such looser forms of comedy as were the outcome of Heywood's *Interludes*, into either of which contemporary allusions and jests could be readily introduced. Nevertheless, the majority of such pieces continued to deal with subjects taken from Roman and Greek mythology, the various anachronisms and absurdities which arose from this method of treatment only contributing to heighten the amusement of the spectators.

I have already implied that *Narcissus* belongs to the class of University plays, inasmuch as it was acted at S. John's College, Oxford, on Twelfth Night, 1602. It does not, however, approximate in any way to the classical form of comedy ; it is rather to be regarded as a Christmas piece, an imitation of the Yule-tide mummeries acted by disguised villagers or townsfolk at the houses of such wealthier persons as would afford them hospitality.

The following list of Oxford plays—compiled, with additions, from W. L. Courtney's article in *Notes and Queries* for December 11th, 1886, and W. Carew Hazlitt's *Manual of English Plays*—may be of interest, as showing the frequency of dramatic entertainments at the various colleges between 1547 and the Restoration. The dates appended are in most cases those of presentation ; but when these are either unknown, or impossible to distinguish from dates of entry at Stationers' Hall, I have substituted the latter.

1547.   *Archipropheta*, sive *Joannes Baptista*, by Nicholas Grimald, in Ch. Ch. Hall.

1566.   *Marcus Geminus*, by (?) in Ch. Ch. Hall.

1566.   *Palæmon and Arcyte*, by Richard Edwards, in Ch. Ch. Hall.

1566.   *Ariosto*, by Geo. Gascoigne, at Trin. Coll.

1566.   *Progne*, by Dr. James Calfhill, in Ch. Ch. Hall.

? 1580.   *Ulysses Redux*, by William Gager, in Ch. Ch. Hall.

1581.   *Meleager*, by William Gager, in Ch. Ch. Hall.

1582.   *Supposes*, translated from Ariosto, by Geo. Gascoigne, at Trin. Coll.

xiii

1582. *Julius Cæsar,* by Dr. Geddes, in Ch. Ch. Hall.

1583. *Rivales,* by William Gager, in Ch. Ch. Hall.

1583. *Dido,* by William Gager, in Ch. Ch. Hall.

? *Tancred,* by H. Wotton, at Queen's Coll.

? *Kermophus,* by George Wild (?) at (?)

1591. *Kynes Redux,* by William Gager, in Ch. Ch. Hall.

1592. *Bellum Grammaticale,* sive *Nominum Verborumque Discordia Civilis,* by (?) at Ch. Ch.

? 1602. *Hamlet,* by W. Shakspere, at (?).

1602. *Narcissus,* by (?) at S. John's College.

1605. *Ajax Flagellifer,* by (?) at (?).

1605. *Alba,* by (?) in Ch. Ch. Hall.

1605. *Vertumnus,* sive, *Annus Recurrens Oxonii,* by Dr. Matthew Gwinne, in Ch. Ch. Hall.

1606. *The Queen's Arcadia,* by Samuel Daniel, in Ch. Ch. Hall.

1607. *Cæsar and Pompey,* by (?) at Trin. Coll.

1607. *The Christmas Prince,* by divers hands, at S. John's Coll.

1608. *Yule-tide,* by (?) at Ch. Ch.

1614. *Spurius,* by Peter Heylin, at Hart Hall.

1617. *Technogamia,* by Barten Holiday, at Ch. Ch.

1617-8. *Philosophaster,* by R. Burton, at Ch. Ch.

1631. *The Raging Turk,* by Thomas Goffe, at Ch. Ch.

1632. *The Courageous Turk,* by Thomas Goffe, at Ch. Ch.

1633. *Fuimus Troes,* by Dr. Jasper Fisher, at Magd. Coll.

1633. *Orestes,* by Thomas Goffe, at Ch. Ch.

? 1634. *The Sophister,* by R. Zouch, at (?).

1634-5. *Euphormus*, sive, *Cupido Adultus*, by Geo. Wilde, at S. John's Coll.

1636. *Stonehenge*, by John Speed, at S. John's Coll.

1636. *The floating Island*, by William Strode, at Ch. Ch.

1636. *Love's Hospital* (or, *The Hospital of Lovers*), by Geo. Wilde, at S. John's Coll.

1636. *The Royal Slave*, by William Cartwright, at Ch. Ch.

1637. *The Converted Robber*, by Geo. Wilde, at S. John's College.

? 1640. *Pharamus*, sive, *Libido Vindex* (also published under the title of *Thibaldus*, sive *Vindictæ Ingenium*), by Thomas Snelling, at (?).

1648. *Stoicus Vapulans*, by (?) at S. John's Coll.

1648. *Amorous War*, by Jasper Maine, D.D., at (?).

? *The Scholar*, by Richard Lovelace, at Gloucester Hall. (Prologue and Epilogue appear in *Lucasta*, 1649.)

1651. *The Lady Errant*, by William Cartwright, at (?).

1653. *The Inconstant Lady*, by Arthur Wilson, at Trin. Coll. (?)

1654. *The Combat of Love and Friendship*, by Robt. Mead, at Ch. Ch.

1660. *The Christmas Ordinary*, by W. R., M.A., at Trin. Coll.

1660. *The Guardian*, by (?) at "new dancing-school against S. Michael's Church." (Wood, iii. 705.)

1663. *Flora's Vagaries*, by Richard Rhodes, at Ch. Ch.

This catalogue does not, of course, pretend to be exhaustive. An examination of the various college archives would doubtless afford further material. There exists, for instance, the record of performances at Merton; cf. G. C. Brodrick's *Memorials of Merton College* (Oxford Hist. Soc., 1885), p. 67 : " In January and February, 1566-7, two dramatic performances were given in the Warden's lodgings by members of the foundation . . . . the one being an English comedy, and the other Terence's *Eunuchus*. . . . . Again, in 1568, a play of Plautus was acted in the hall."

It will be seen that of the above-mentioned plays six, besides *Narcissus*, were performed at the College of S. John the Baptist, the first recorded being the *Christmas Prince* in 1607, the succeeding ones taking place after an interval of twenty-six years ; and to these we should very probably add *Pharamus*, the writer of which, Thomas Snelling, " became Scholar of S. John's in 1633, aged 19, and afterwards fellow . . . . and was esteemed an excellent Latin poet." (Wood, *Ath. Ox.*, vol. iii., p. 275.)

A passage from Wake's *Rex Platonicus* (ed. 1, p. 18) is also worthy of note in this connection : "Quorum primos jam ordines dum principes contemplantur, primisque congratulantium acclamationibus delectantur, Collegium Diui Iohannis, nobile literarum domicilium (quod Dominus Thomas Whitus Prætor olim Londinensis, opimis reditibus locupletârat) faciles eorum oculos speciosæ structuræ adblanditione invitat ; moxque et oculos & aures detinet ingeniosâ nec injucundâ lusiunculâ quâ clarissimus præses cum quinquaginta, quos alit Collegium studiosis, magnaque studentium conuiventium cateruâ prodeuns, principes in transitu salutandos censuit.

"Fabulæ ansam dedit antiqua de Regia prosapia historiola apud Scoto-Britannos celebrata, quæ narrat tres olim Sibyllas occurrisse duobus Scotiæ proceribus Macbetho & Banchoni, & illum prædixisse Regem futurum, sed Regem nullum geniturum, hunc Regem non futurum, sed Reges geniturum multos. Vaticinii veritatem rerum eventus comprobavit: Banchonis enim è stirpe Potentissimus Iacobus oriundus. Tres adolescentes concinno Sibyllarum habitu induti, è Collegio prodeuntes, & carmina lepida alternatim canentes, Regi se tres esse illas Sibyllas profitentur, quæ Banchoni olim Sobolis imperia prædixerant, jamque iterum comparere, vt eâdem vaticinij veritate prædicerent Iacobo, se iam, & diu regem futurum Britanniæ felicissimum & multorum Regum parentem, vt ex Banchonis stirpe nunquam sit hæres Britannico diademati defuturus. Deinde tribus Principibus suaves felicitatum triplicitates triplicatis carminum vicibus succinentes veniamque precantes, quòd alumni ædium Divi Iohannis (qui præcursor Christi) alumnos Ædis Christi (quo tum Rex tendebat) præcursoriâ hâc salutatione antevertissent, Principes ingeniosâ fictiunculâ delectatos dimittunt; quos inde vniversa astantium multitudo, felici prædictionum successui suffragans, votis precibusque ad portam vsque civitatis Borealem prosequitur."

The *Christmas Prince* is, properly speaking, not a single play, but a collection of performances consequent on the revival of the old custom, left in abeyance since 1577, of choosing a prince, or master of the revels, who should exercise undisputed authority during the festive season, and in whose honour the company at large should indulge freely in various sorts of pastimes. The account given of this revival, in 1607, seems to imply that there had been of late years no Christmas festivities at S. John's. In 1602 the college porter, pleading for the admission of players on Twelfth Night, could say :

> " Christmas is now at the point to bee past ;
> 'Tis giving vp the ghost and this is the last ;
> And shall it passe thus without life or cheere ?
> This hath not beene seene this many a yeere."

Without laying too much stress upon a single allusion, it is safe to assert that the discovery of the comedy of *Narcissus*, played five years earlier than the performances of which an account is given in the *Christmas Prince*, must be of considerable interest in the history of S. John's, and indeed in that of Oxford play-acting generally.

The MS. containing this comedy is one of the Rawlinson collection, now in the possession of the Bodleian Library. The volume, which is $5\frac{1}{2}$ × 4 inches in size, with 156 leaves, appears to have been the common-place book of an Oxford man. It contains a variety of English poems and prose pieces, written at the end of the sixteenth and beginning of the seventeenth century; amongst them several pages of extracts from the essays of Bacon and of his less-known contemporary Robert Johnson. Sir H. Wotton's poem, " How happy is he borne or taught," also finds a place in the collection. But the majority of the contents are of small literary value, and, so far as I am aware, have never been published. Perhaps the most interesting pieces in the volume are certain " English Epigrammes much like Buckminster's Almanacke . . . . calculated by John Davis of Grayes Inne . . . . 1594 " of the character of which the follow-

ing lines, occurring early in the series, may give some
idea.

> " Oft in my laughinge rimes I name a gull,
> But this new tearme will many questions breed,
> Therefore at first I will describe at full
> Who is a true & perfect gull indeede.
>
> " A gull is hee that weares a velvett gowne,
> And when a wench is brave dare not speake to her ;
> A gull is hee that traverseth the towne,
> And is for marriage knowne a common wooer.
>
> " A gull is hee that, when he proudly weares
> A silver hilted rapier by his side,
> Endures the lye and knocks about the eares,
> Whilst in his sheath his sleepinge sword doth bide.
>
> " A gull is hee that hath good handsome cloaths,
> And stands in presence stroking vpp his haire,
> And fills vpp his imperfecte speech with oathes,
> But speaks not one wise woord throughout the yeere.
> But, to define a gull in tearms precise,
> A gull is hee that seemes, and is not, wise."

That the play now under consideration is the work of
some member or members of the college of S. John's
there can be no doubt. It is, as the Prologue affirms,
" Ovid's owne Narcissus," *i.e.*, the story of Narcissus as
told in the third book of the *Metamorphoses*, which forms
the basis of the plot ; and the resemblance to the Latin is
in parts so close as necessarily to imply a knowledge of
that language on the part of the writer. There is, indeed,
one passage of literal and yet graceful translation (see
ll. 494-505) which especially betokens a scholarly hand.

But it has been already hinted that the chief interest
of the comedy lies in another direction. The arrange-
ment and methods are those of the rough-and-ready

xix

English stage of the period; and as in the Pyramus and Thisbe interlude of the *Midsummer Night's Dream*, and the Nine Worthies of *Love's Labour's Lost*, the writer imitates and ridicules that naïve realism which appertained to native comedy in its rude embryonic forms. The absurdities with which the *Narcissus* abounds are obviously intentional; it is, in fact, a burlesque, not skilful nor humorous enough to take its place beside the immortal parodies of Shakspere, which in aim and scope it resembles, but a good average specimen of its class, doubtless provocative of intense delight in the minds of a contemporary audience. It is, of course, with a view to heightening the reality of the effect that the Porter is made to plead on behalf of certain "youths of the parish," who are waiting, armed with their wassail-bowl, for admittance into the hall, and who, besides a song, have "some other sporte too out of dowbt" for the delectation of the assembled guests. Then follows, first the song, and afterwards an altercation in prose between the Porter and the Players, who assume an air of bashfulness when called upon to exercise their dramatic talent. Finally, the Prologue enters, and the play is begun; the general smoothness of the versification standing out in contrast to the intentional doggerel of the Porter's introductory speech and epilogue.

The mention of "youths of the parish" is probably not serious; but as an allusion to a real play of the kind here imitated, the following extract from the *Christmas Prince* (ed. 1816, p. 25) may be of interest: "S. Steevens day was past over in silence, and so had S. John's day also; butt that some of the princes honest neighbours of S. Giles presented him with a maske or morris, which though it were but rudely performed, yet itt being so

freely & lovingly profered it could not but bee as lovingly
received."

I shall now pass on to the consideration of the play
itself, and, first, of the characters which make up the list
of *dramatis personæ*.   Five of these, namely, Tiresias,
Cephisus, Narcissus, Echo, and Liriope, appear in the
story of Narcissus as told by Ovid.   Cephisus, son of
Pontus and Thalassa, and divinity of the river whence
he derives his name, is the father of the hero ; the nymph
Liriope is his mother.   Tiresias, the blind prophet of
Thebes, and Echo, the unhappy victim of the anger of
Juno and the contempt of Narcissus, are well-known
figures in classical mythology.   Neither Dorastus and
Clinias, who attend Narcissus as youthful friends, nor
Florida and Clois, nymphs enamoured of his beauty, have
any actual counterparts in the *Metamorphoses*.

Most curious and interesting is the inclusion of " The
Well" in the list of characters.   We have here no mere
stage property, or piece of scenery, but an actual personi-
fication of an inanimate object, closely resembling that
of Wall and Moonshine in Peter Quince's company.
Just as Moonshine carries a lantern to represent more
vividly the actual moon, so the personage called The Well
aids the imagination of his audience by the visible sign
of a water-bucket   The fact of his being enumerated
amongst the *dramatis personæ* shows that the part was
played by a separate artist, and not doubled with that of
any other character.   Of the Porter, Francis, more will be
said in Section II.

The play of *Narcissus*, though it can boast of no
artificial divisions, falls naturally into twelve different

portions, which for want of a better term I will call scenes. Whilst using this word it is necessary to bear in mind that no change of *scenery* is implied, and probably none was intended.

Scene I. reveals Cephisus, Liriope, and Narcissus, awaiting the prophet Tiresias. It consists of 132 lines, amplified from *Met.* iii. 341, 346-348 :

> " Prima fide vocisque ratæ tentamina sumsit
> Cærula Liriope . . . .
> . . . . De quo consultus, an esset
> Tempora maturæ visurus longa senectæ
> Fatidicus vates—' Si se non viderit ' inquit."

The introduction of Cephisus, the conversation between Narcissus and his parents, the telling of the youth's fate *by the aid of chiromancy*, and Liriope's scornful comment on the prophecy, are the materials used by the English writer to form an effective scene.

Scene II. is wholly an interpolation. Dorastus and Clinias also try their fate with Tiresias ; he prophesies their early death, and they jest upon the subject.

Scene III., in which Dorastus and Clinias flatter Narcissus for his beauty, has no counterpart in Ovid. Probably, however, it was suggested by *Met.* iii. 353-355 :

> " Multi illum juvenes, multæ cupiere puellæ ;
> Sed fuit in tenera tam dira superbia forma ;
> Nulli illum juvenes, nullæ tetigere puellæ."

Scene IV. pursues a like theme ; the nymphs Florida and Clois are in their turn repulsed by the scornful youth, and relate their woes to Dorastus and Clinias.

The hint for this is given in *Met.* iii. 402 :

> " Sic hanc, sic alias undis aut montibus ortas
> Luserat hic Nymphas."

And likewise the suggestion of Florida's revengeful wish :

> " Inde manus aliquis despectus ad æthera tollens
> ' Sic amet ipse licet, sic non potiatur amato ! '
> Dixerat."

Scene V. Echo enters, and gives an account of herself, amplified—with a very free use of the English vernacular —from *Met.* iii. 356-368.

Scene VI., which has no counterpart in Ovid, consists of a spirited hunting-song in five stanzas, sung (presumably) while Narcissus, Dorastus, and Clinias chase a supposed hare over the stage.

Scene VII. introduces the "one with a bucket," *i.e.,* The Well. The first twelve lines of his speech are a literal and smoothly-versified translation of *Met.* iii. 407-412. In Ovid, however, this description of the well comes after the conversation between Echo and Narcissus, and the account proceeds at once (l. 413) with :

> " Hic puer, et studio venandi lassus et æstu,
> Procubuit."

It is doubtful why the English writer should have preferred to introduce the Well thus early. With Ovid's lines may be compared those in the translation of the *Romaunt of the Rose* attributed to Chaucer :

> " —— Springyng in a marble stone,
> Had nature set the sothe to tel
> Under that pyne tree a wel.
> .   .   .   .   .   .
> Aboute it is grasse springyng
> For moyste so thycke and wel lykyng,
> That it ne may in wynter dye
> No more than may the see be drye.
> .   .   .   .   .   .
> For of the welle this is the syne,

In worlde is none so clere of hewe,
The water is euer fresshe and newe
That welmeth vp with wawes bright."

Scene VIII. consists of a dialogue between Dorastus and Echo.

Scene IX. continues the same theme, Clinias being substituted for Dorastus. Both these scenes are interpolations, introduced evidently for the amusement of the audience rather than for any bearing on the main plot.

Scene X. Here Narcissus delivers himself of a soliloquy, suggested by *Met.* iii. 479 :

" Forte puer, comitum seductus et agmine fido,
Dixerat "—

He is answered by Echo, who wishes to proffer him her affection. The conversation, gathered from Ovid, runs as follows :

" Ecquis adest ?
Adest.
Veni !
Veni !
Quid me fugis ?
Quid me fugis ?
Huc Coëamus !
Coeämus ! "

This, with various amplifications, is followed in ll. 602-630 of the *Narcissus.*

Here, however, there is no reproduction of Ovid's account :

" Et verbis favet ipsa suis, egressaque silvis
Ibat, ut injiceret sperato brachia collo.
Ille fugit, fugiensque manus complexibus aufert."

which leads on to and explains the next speech of Narcissus :

" 'Ante' ait 'emoriar, quam sit tibi copia nostri.'"

rendered in the English by :

"Let mee dye first ere thou meddle with mee."

This terminates the interview; Echo does not seem to make any appearance on the stage. The few lines which, in Ovid, describe the effect of her hopeless love, are partly followed in ll. 740-747 of the English play.

Scene XI. Dorastus and Clinias abuse, fight with, and finally kill each other.

Scene XII. Narcissus enters, *fleeing from Echo* (a connecting touch not found in Ovid). His speech, on discovering the well, is a mixture of the description of his transports in the *Metamorphoses*, and of the soliloquy there attributed to him. ll. 697-707 of the *Narcissus* correspond word for word to *Met.* iii. 442-450.

It is remarkable that the use of the name of the goddess of corn instead of bread itself (" Cereris," l. 437) should have suggested to the English writer a similar metaphorical use of the names of Morpheus and Bacchus. Another small point worthy of note is the introduction of a jest into the midst of this mournful scene; Ovid's :

> " Et, quantum motu formosi suspicor oris,
> Verba refers aures non pervenientia nostras "

being irreverently rendered by :

> " And by thy lippes moving, well I doe suppose
> Woordes thou dost speake, may well come to our nose ;
> For to oure eares I am sure they never passe."

Ovid's Narcissus discovers his own identity with the vision (*Met.* iii. 463), which the English version ignores ; while, on the other hand, the prophecy of ll. 730-731 :

> " I, which whilome was
> The flower of youth, shalbee made flower againe "

finds no counterpart in Ovid.

d

Many of the reflections and entreaties ascribed to Narcissus in the Latin version are omitted in the English ; neither is there any mention of the beating of the breast (*Met.* iii. 480-485). The final conversation with Echo is given thus by Ovid :

> Eheu !
> Eheu !
> Heu frustra dilecte puer !
> Heu frustra dilecte puer !
> Vale !
> Vale !

The English writer somewhat amplifies this, Echo being always a favourite stage-character. The rising up of Narcissus after death is an English expedient; so is Echo's return to give a final account of herself, the matter of which is suggested, as has been said, by *Met.* iii. 393-401.

So much for the classical basis of the play; it remains to notice briefly the points in which it resembles an English comedy, or shows traces of the influence of other English writers. Most remarkable in the latter connection is the frequent coincidence of expressions between the *Narcissus* and Shakspere's *Henry IV.* (Part I.). Amongst these are the following :

L. 78.	Ladds of metall.	Cf. 1 *Henry IV.*,	ii. 4,	13.
80.	No vertue extant	„	ii. 4,	132.
111.	I tickle (them) for	„	ii. 4,	489.
422.	Never ioyd (it) since	„	ii. 1,	13.
575.	Kee (= quoth) pickpurse	„	ii. 1,	53.
734.	(My) grandam earth	„	iii. 1,	34.

See also the notes on ll. 282, 396, and 683.

As *Henry IV.* was entered at Stationers' Hall February 25th, 1597, and the first quarto appeared in 1598, it is quite possible that these may be direct borrowings on the part of the writer of the *Narcissus.*

A common trick of English burlesque at this time (cf. *Midsummer Night's Dream*, v. 1, 337, etc.) was the inversion of epithets, producing nonsensical combinations; an expedient which, if we condemn it as poor wit, we must at least allow to fall under the definition of humour as "the unexpected." A good example of this occurs in ll. 360, 361 :

> "So cruell as the huge camelion,
> Nor yet so changing as small elephant."

And another in ll. 677, 678 :

> "But oh, remaine, and let thy christall lippe
> No more of this same cherrye water sippe."

Sarcastic allusions are also not wanting; see, for instance, the cheerful inducement held out to Narcissus :

> "As true as Helen was to Menela,
> So true to you will bee thy Florida."

And cf. the notes on ll. 337, 342.

There are several facetious mistakes in the forms of words, such as *spoone* for moon (l. 350), *Late-mouse* for Latmus (l. 279), and *Davis* for Davus (l. 400) ; of which the first recalls Ancient Pistol's "Cannibals" (2 *Henry IV*. ii. 4, 180), or the contrary slip in *Every Man in his Humour*, iii. 4, 53, and the two latter, Bottom's "Shafalus" and "Procrus," and the blunders of Costard.

The naïve devices by which the players seem to have made up for some paucity of accoutrements and stage appliances, and their direct appeals to the intelligence of the audience to excuse all defects, are highly edifying. There is, as I have before remarked, no indication of any scenery ; and the only characters whom we know to have worn a special dress are Tiresias and Liriope. The prophets of classical history were often converted into bishops by English writers; so, for example, Helenus, son of Priam, in the fourteenth century alliterative *Gest Hystoriale of Troy*. This is why Tiresias wears a bishop's rochet. It is unfortunate that the collection of robes now in the possession of St. John's College does not include a garment of this description.

Liriope has a symbolical costume, which she very carefully interprets to Narcissus:

> " And I thy mother nimphe, as may bee seene
> By coulours that I weare, blew, white, and greene;
> For nimphes ar of the sea, and sea is right
> Of coulour truly greene and blew and white.
> Would you knowe how, I pray? Billowes are blew,
> Water is greene, and foome is white of hue."

Cephisus is content to carry the emblems of his origin, which he emphasizes at the same time by representative action:

> " Thy father I, Cephisus, that brave river
> Who is all water, doe like water shiver.
> As any man of iudgment may descrye
> By face, hands washt, and bowle, thy father I."

In the same way Narcissus, rising up after his supposed death, bears a daffodil as a sign of his metamorphosis, addressing the audience after a manner more brusque than polite:

> " If you take mee for Narcissus y'are very sillye,
> I desire you to take mee for a daffa downe dillye;
> For so I rose, and so I am in trothe,
> As may appeare by the flower in my mouthe."

Echo gives her reasons somewhat confidentially:

> " But ho, the hobby horse, youle think't absurde
> That I should of my selfe once speake a woord.
> 'Tis true; but lett your wisdomes tell me than,
> How'de you know Eccho from another man?"

And at the conclusion of the play she kindly directs the imagination of the spectators into the right channel :

> " Now auditors of intelligence quicke,
> I pray you suppose that Eccho is sicke "——

and craves their applause by a skilful ruse.

Tiresias makes his exit at an early stage in the play, addressing congratulations to himself :

> " Goe, thou hast done, Tyresias ; bidd adieu ;
> Thy part is well plaid and thy wordes are true."

As a last instance of this naïve custom, Florida's words at the end of the short part assigned to herself and Clois may be cited :

> " Looke you for maids no more, our parte is done,
> Wee come but to be scornd, and so are gone."

Both the songs contained in the play have a considerable amount of vivacity and vigour, though they fall short of actual lyrical beauty. The first and longer of the two is a drinking-song with a refrain of eight lines, written in a lively and irregular, but not ill-handled metre ; the second, a hunting-song of five stanzas, with the chorus "Yolp" in imitation of the cry of the dogs. Besides these, which may very possibly have been in existence before the play was written, the effusion of Dorastus on meeting Narcissus (" Cracke eye strings cracke," l. 305) is lyrical in character.

Taken as a whole, it will be seen that the comedy of *Narcissus* is rather interesting for its quaintness, its humour, and its apparent borrowings from, and undoubted resemblances to, Shakspere, than for any intrinsic literary value. In spite of this, I cannot but hope that those who now study it for the first time, though they may have "seene a farre better play at the theater," will not find reason to condemn it as wholly dull and unprofitable.

SECTION II.

It only remains to say a few words with regard to the four pieces which I have included in the present volume. These occur in the same MS. as the *Narcissus*, and taken with it appear to form a united group, by virtue of their common connection with S. John's College. It is true that the Porter who acts so prominent a part in the admission of the supposed players reveals to us only his Christian name, Frances (see last line of Epilogue), but it is hardly possible to doubt his identity with the Francke (or Francis) Clarke, the porter of S. John's, to whom the remarkable productions above-mentioned are attributed. After several vain attempts to discover the record of this man's tenure of office, I have chanced upon his name in Mr. A. Clark's *Register of the University of Oxford*, vol. ii. (1571-1622), pt. 1, p. 398, where it occurs in the list of "personæ privilegiatæ," a term including, in its widest sense, all persons who enjoyed the immunities conferred by charter on the corporation of the University, but technically used to describe certain classes to whom these immunities were granted by special favour; as, for example, the college servants, of whom the manciple, cook, and porter or janitor, were amongst the chief.

The entry is as follows:

" 8 May 1601, S. Jo., Clark, Francis; Worc., pleb. f., 24; 'janitor.'"

From this we gather that Francis Clark had not been

long appointed to his office; that he was twenty-four years of age, a Worcestershire man, and of humble birth.

Judging by the internal evidence of the MS. now under consideration, we may very naturally suppose that the porter, a worthy possessed of a shrewd wit and somewhat combative temperament, enjoyed high favour amongst the undergraduates, though often in disgrace with their superiors; and that for his benefit (in the case of the first and fourth pieces), and for their own (in the case of the third), the wags of the college composed certain apologies, which Francis Clarke was clever enough to commit to memory, and confident enough to pronounce before the Head in the character of a privileged humourist. The last of the pieces seems to have been written down and delivered as a letter; and some or all may be the products of the same pen as wrote the *Narcissus*. That they were not written by the porter himself is evident; for over and above the mere improbability that a college servant would be capable of such frequent reference to Lilly, we have the testimony of the headings, two of which bear mention of "a speech *made for* the foresaid porter," and "a letter *composed for* Francke Clarke." It is very possible that the porter's part in the *Narcissus* may have been specially designed for, and entrusted to, the worthy Francis.

Of these four pieces, the apology addressed to "Master President, that had sconc't him 10 groates for letting the fidlers into the hall at Christmas," occurs next to the play in the MS., and was probably the result of some mock trial and sentence forming a part of the Christmas festivities. If we could suppose the "fidlers" to have been the same as the players, a still closer connection would be established between this speech and the comedy; but there is no mention of any dramatic entertainment in the circumstantial account of their entrance and exit given by the porter.

The other pieces have no apparent connection with Christmas time, and the last, being addressed to Laud during the year of his proctorship, fixes its own date as 1603-4. The speech *To the Ladie Keneda* is the most puzzling of the group, inasmuch as it bears no reference to collegiate life, and deals with a subject of some obscurity. *Kennedy* was the family name of the earls of Cassilis; and the fifth earl, then living, had married in 1597 Jean, daughter of James, fourth Lord Fleming, and widow of Lord Chancellor Maitland. But whether she is the "Ladie Keneda" to whom Francis Clarke pleads on behalf of her cook Piers, it is impossible to say. Neither have I found out anything concerning the annual holiday for cooks, to which allusion seems to be made. Here, however, as in the other speeches, a wide margin must be allowed for euphuism, and bare facts are difficult to deduce.

I have refrained from supplying references to the numerous classical quotations with which the speeches are embellished, for the simple reason that a contemporary edition of Lilly's Grammar will be found to include them all. Doubtless the youthful composers derived a special delight from the process of making " Lilly leape out of his skinne," with a " muster of sentences " of which the porter's supposed use and interpretation is, if not always scholarly, at least decidedly ingenious.

A

TWELFE NIGHT MERRIMENT.

Anno 1602.

Enter the Porter *at the end of supper.*

Porter.

ASTER and Mistris with all your guests,   F. 81ᵛ rcv.
God save you, heerin the matter rests ;
Christmas is now at the point to bee
        past,
'Tis giving vp the ghost & this is the
        last ;
And shall it passe thus without life or cheere ?
This hath not beene seene this many a yeere.
If youl have any sporte, then say the woord,
Heere come youths of the parish that will it affoord,
They are heere hard by comminge alonge,
Crowning their wassaile bowle with a songe :   10
They have some other sport too out of dowbt,
Let mee alone, & I will finde it out.
I am your porter & your vassaile,
Shall I lett in the boyes with their wassaile ?

I

B

Say: they are at doore, to sing they beginne,
Goe to then, Ile goe & lett them in !

Enter the wassaile, two of them bearinge the bowle, &
singinge the songe, & all of them bearing the burden.

The Songe.

Gentills all
Both great & small,
Sitt close in the hall
    And make some roome,

20

For amongst you heere
At the end of your cheere
With our countrey beare
    Wee ar bold to come.
        Heers then a full carowse,
        Let it goe about the house,
        While wee doe carrye it thus
          'Tis noe great labour.
        Heave it vpp merilye,

F. 81ʳ rev.

30

        Let care & anger flye,
        A pinne for povertye ;
          Drinke to your neighbour.

Those that are wise,
Doe knowe that with spice
God Bacchus his iuyce
    Is wholsome & good.
It comforts age,
It refresheth the sage,
It rebateth rage,

40

    And cheereth the bloud.
        Heeres then a full, &c.

2

Take it with quicknes,
Tis phisicke for sicknes,
It driveth the thicknes
    Of care from the harte ;
The vaynes that are empty
It filleth with plenty,
Not one amongst twenty
    But it easeth of smarte.
        Heers then a full, &c.   50

Are you sadd,
For fortune badd,
And would bee gladd
    As ever you were,
If that a quaffe
Doe not make you laffe,
Then with a staffe
    Drive mee out of dore.
        Heers then a full, &c.

To tell you his merritts,   60
Good thoughts it inherites,
It raiseth the spirritts
    And quickens the witt ;
It peoples the veyns,
It scoureth the reynes,
It purgeth the braines
    And maks all things fitte.
        Heers then a full, &c.

It makes a man bold,
It keepes out the cold ;   70
Hee hath all things twice told
    Vnto his comforte,

Hee stands in the middle,
The world, hey dery diddle,
Goes round without a fiddle
To make them sporte.
Heers then a full carowse, &c.

Por. Why well said, my ladds of mettall, this is som-
what yett, 'tis trimlye done ; but what sporte, what merri-
80 ment, all dead, no vertue extant ?

Pri[mus]. Pray, sir, gett our good Mistris to bestowe
something on us, & wee ar gone.

Por. Talke of that *tempore venturo ;* there's no goinge
to any other houses now, your bowle is at the bottome,
& that which is left is for mee.

Sec[undus]. Nay, good Master Porter.

Por. Come, come, daunce vs a morrice, or els goe sell
fishe ; I warrant youle make as good a night of it heere
as if you had beene at all the houses in the towne.

90 *Ter[tius].* Nay, pray letts goe, wee can doe nothinge.

Por. Noe! What was that I tooke you all a gabling
tother day in mother Bunches backside by the well there,
when Tom at Hobses ranne vnder the hovell with a kettle
on's head ?

Pri. Why, you would not have a play, would you ?

Por. Oh, by all meanes, 'tis your onely fine course.
About it, ladds, a the stampe, I warrante you a reward
sufficient; I tell you, my little windsuckers, had not a
certaine melancholye ingendred with a nippinge dolour
100 overshadowed the sunne shine of my mirthe, I had beene
I pre, sequor, one of your consorte.   But wheres gooddy
Hubbardes sonne—I saw him in his mothers holliday
cloaths eennow ?

Sec. Doe you heere, Master Porter, wee have pittifull

4

nailes in our shooes; you were best lay something on the grounde, els wee shall make abhominable scarrs in the face on't.

Por. *Rem tenes;* well, weele thinke on't.

Ter. It is a most condolent tragedye wee shall move.

Por. *Dictum puta; satis est quod suffocat.*   110

Sec. In faith, I tickle them for a good voice.

Por. *Sufficiente quantitate,* a woord is enough to the wise.

Pri. You have noe butterd beare in the house, have ·yee?

Por. No, no, trudge, some of the guests are one the point to bee gone.

Sec. Have you ere a gentlewomans picture in the house, or noe?

Por. Why?   120

Sec. If you have, doe but hange it yonder, & twill make mee act in conye.

Por. Well then, away about your geere.

                          [Exeunt.

Enter Prologue.

Wee are noe vagabones, wee ar no arrant
   Rogues that doe runne with plaies about the country.
Our play is good, & I dare farther warrant   F. 79ʳ rev.
  It will make you more sport then catt in plum tree.
      Wee are no saucye common playenge skipiackes,
      But towne borne lads, the kings owne lovely
         subiects.

This is the night, night latest of the twelve,   130
   Now give vs leave for to bee blith & frolicke,

To morrow wee must fall to digg & delve;
   Weele bee but short, long sittinge breeds the collicke.
      Then wee beginne, & lett none hope to hisse vs,
      The play wee play is Ovid's owne Narcissus.

[*Cep.*] Open thine eares, my sonne, open I bidd
To heare the sound saw which the sage shall reed,
I meane the sage Tyresias, my ducke,
Which shall lay ope to thee thy lott, thy lucke.
140 Thy father I, Cephisus, that brave river
Who is all water, doe like water shiver.
As any man of iudgment may descrye
By face, hands washt, & bowle, thy father I.
   Lyr. And I thy mother nimphe, as may bee seene
By coulours that I weare, blew, white, & greene;
For nimphes ar of the sea, & sea is right
Of colour truly greene & blew & white;
Would you knowe how, I pray? Billowes are blew,
Water is greene, & foome is white of hue.
150   *Cep.* Wee both bidd the, Narcisse, our dearest child,
With count'nance sober, modest lookes & milde,
To prophett's wisest woords with tention harken;
But Sunne is gonne & welkin gins to darken,
Vulcan the weary horses is a shooinge,
While Phebus with queene Thetis is a doinge:
Prophett comes not, letts goe both all & some,
Wee may goe home like fooles as wee did come.
   Lyr. O stay deare husband, flowe not away bright
      water,
The prophett will come by sooner or later.

6

Cep. Why stand wee heere, as it were cappes a 160
   thrumming,
To look for prophett? Prophett is not comminge.
   Nar. Sweete running river which Cephisus hight,
Whose water is so cleare, whose waves so bright,
Gold is thy sand and christall is thy current,
Thy brooke so cleare that no vile wind dare stirre in't;
Thou art my father, & thou, sweetest nimphe,
Thou art my mother, I thy sonne, thy shrimpe.
Agree you in one point, to goe or tarrye,
Narcissus must obey, aye, must hee, marye.
   Cep. Gush, water, gush! runne, river, from thy channell! 170
Thou hast a sonne more lovinge then a spanniell;
With watry eyes I see how tis expedient
To have a sonne so wise & so obedient.
Most beauteous sonne, yet not indeede so beautifull
As thou art mannerly & dutifull!
   Lyr. See, husband, see, O see where prophett blind
In twice good time is comming heere behind.
   Cep. O heere hee is, and now that hee's come nye vs,
Lye close, good wife & sonne, least hee espye vs.

Enter TYRESIAS.

All you that see mee heere in byshoppes rochett, F. 78ʳ rev.
180
And I see not, your heads may runne on crotchett,
For ought I knowe, to knowe what manner wight
In this strange guise I am, or how I hight;
I am Tyresias, the not seeing prophett,
Blinde though I bee, I pray lett noe man scoffe it:
For blind I am, yea, blind as any beetle,
And cannot see a whitt, no, nere so little.

7

Heere ar no eyes, why, they ar in my minde,
Wherby I see the fortunes of mankind ;
190 Who made mee blind ? Jove ? I may say to you noe ;
But it was Joves wife & his sister Juno.
Juno & Jove fell out, both biggest gods,
And I was hee tooke vpp the merrye oddes.
You knowe it all, I am sure, 'tis somewhat common,
And how besides seven yeares I was a woman ;
Which if you knowe you doe know all my state :
Come on, Ile fold the fortune of your fate.
  Lyr. Tremblinge, Tyresias, I pray you cease to travell,
And rest a little on the groundy gravell.
200 *Tyr.* Who ist calls ? Speake, for I cannot see.
  Cep. Poore frends, sir, to the number of some three.
  Tyr. What would you have ?
  Cep. Why, sir, this is the matter,
To bee plaine with you & not to flatter ;
I am the stately river hight Cephise,
Smoother then glasse & softer farre then ice ;
This nimphe before you heere whom you doe see
Is my owne wife, yclipt Lyriope.
Though with the dawbe of prayse I am loath to lome her,
210 This Ile assure you, the blind poett Homer
Saw not the like amongst his nimphes and goddesses,
Nor in his Iliads, no, nor in his Odysses.
Thinke not, I pray, that wee are come for nought ;
Our lovely infant have wee to you brought.
The purple hew of this our iolly striplynge
I would not have you thinke was gott with tiplinge ;
Hee is our sonne Narcisse, no common varlett,
Nature in graine hath died his face in skarlett.
Speak then, I pray you, speake, for wee you portune
220 That you would tell our sunnfac't sonne his fortune.

Lyr. Doe not shrink backe, Narcissus, come & stand,
Hold vpp & lett the blind man see thy hand.

Tyr. Come, my young sonne, hold vp & catch audacitye;
I see thy hand with the eyes of my capacitye.
Though I speake riddles, thinke not I am typsye,
For what I speake I learnde it of a gipsye,
And though I speak hard woords of curromanstike,
Doe not, I pray, suppose that I am franticke.
The table of thy hand is somewhat ragged,
Thy mensall line is too direct and cragged,   230
Thy line of life, my sonne, is to, to breife,
And crosseth Venus girdle heere in cheife,
And heere (O dolefull signe) is overthwarte
In Venus mount a little pricke or warte.   F. 77ᵛ rev.
Besides heere, in the hillocke of great Jupiter,
Monnsieur la mors lyes lurking like a sheppbiter;
What can I make out of this hard construction
But dolefull dumpes, decay, death, & destruction?

Cep. O furious fates, O three thread-thrumming sisters,
O fickle fortune, thou, thou art the mistres   240
Of this mishapp; why am I longer liver?
Runne river, runne, & drowne thee in the river.

Tyr. Then sith to thee, my sonne, I doe pronounce ill,
It shall behove thee for to take good counsell,
And that eft soone; wisdoome they say is good,
Your parents ambo have done what they coode,
They can but bringe horse to the water brinke,
But horse may choose whether that horse will drinke.

Lyr. Oh say, thou holy preist of high Apollo,
What harme, what hurt, what chaunge, what chaunce, will 250
    followe,
That if wee can wee may provide a plaster
Of holsome hearbes to cure this dire disaster.

Tyr. If I should tell you, you amisse would iudge it;
I have one salve, one medecine, in my budgett,
And that is this, since you will have mee tell,
If hee himselfe doe never knowe; farewell. [*Exit* TYR.
Lyr. Mary come out, is his ould noddle dotinge?
Heere is an ould said saw well woorth the notinge;
F. 77r rev. Shall hee not know himselfe? Who shall hee then?
My boy shall knowe himselfe from other men,
I, & my boy shall live vntill hee dye,
In spight of prophett & in spight of pye.
It is an ould sawe: That it is too late
When steede is stolne to shutt the stable gate;
Therfore take heed; yet I bethinke at Delph,
One Phibbus walls is written: Knowe thyselfe.
Shall hee not know himselfe, and so bee laught on,
When as Apollo cries, gnotti seauton? [*Exeunt.*

DORASTUS. CLINIAS.

Come, prethy lett vs goe: come, Clinias, come,
And girt thy baskett dagger to thy bumme;
Lett vs, I say, bee packinge, and goe meete
The poore blind prophett stalking in the streete:
Lett us be iogginge quickly.
Cli. Peace, you asse,
I smell the footinge of Tyresias.

Enter TYRESIAS.

Dor. O thou which hast thy staffe to bee thy tutor,
Whose head doth shine with bright hairs white as pewter,
Like silver moone, when as shee kist her minion
In Late-mouse mont, the swaine yclipt Endimion,

Who, beeing cald Endimion the drowsye,
Slept fifty yeers, & for want of shift was lowsye ;
O thou whose breast, I, even this little cantle,
Is counsells capcase, prudences portmantle,
O thou that pickest wisdome out of guttes
As easy as men doe kernells out of nuttes,
Looke in our midriffs, & I pray you tell vs
Whether wee two shall live & dye good fellowes.
    Tyr. How doe you both ?
    Dor. Well, I thanke you.
    Tyr. Are you not sicklye ?   290
    Cli. Noe, I thanke God.
    Tyr. Yet you shall both dye quicklye.
Goe, thou hast done, Tyresias ; bidd adiew ;   [*Exit.*
Thy part is well plaid & thy wordes are true.
    Dor. Shall wee dye quickly, both? I pray what coulour ?
Ile bee a diar, thou shalt be a fuller ;
Weele cozin the prophett, I my life will pawne yee,
Thou shalt dye whyte, & Ile dye oreng tawnye.

       Enter NARCISSUS *walkinge.*
    Cli. O eyes, what see you ? Eyes, bee ever bloud shedd
That turne your Master thus into a codshead.   300
O eyes, noe eyes, O instruments, O engines,
That were ordain'd to worke your Master's vengeance !
His huge orentall beawty melts my eyeballs
Into rayne dropps, even as sunne doth snowballes.
    Dor. Cracke eye strings, cracke,
        Runne eyes, runne backe,
          My lovely brace of beagles ;
        Looke no more on
        Yon shininge sunne,
          For your eyes are not eagles.   310

Leave off the chace
My pretty brace,
   And hide you in your kennell,
And hunt no more,
Your sight is sore ;
   Oh that I had some fennell !

Nar. Leave off to bragg, thou boy of Venus bredd,
I am as faire as thou, for white & redd ;
If then twixt mee & thee theres no more oddes,
320 Why I on earth & thou amongst the goddes ?

   Cli. Thy voice, Narcisse, so softly & so loude,
Makes in mine eares more musicke then a crowde
Of most melodious minstrells, & thy tonge
Is edged with silver, & with iewells strunge ;
Thy throate, which speaketh ever & anan,
Is farre more shriller then the pipe of Pan,
Thy weasand pipe is clearer then an organ,
Thy face more faire then was the head of Gorgon,
Thy haire, which bout thy necke so faire dishevells,
330 Excells the haire of the faire queene of devills,
And thy perfumed breath farr better savours
Then does the sweat hot breath of blowing Mavors ;
Thy azur'd veynes blewer then Saturne shine,

And what are Cupids eyes to those of thine ?
Thy currall cheeks hath a farre better lustre
Then Ceres when the sunne in harvest bust her ;
Silenus for streight backe, & I can tell yee,
You putt downe Bacchus for a slender bellye.
To passe from braunch to barke, from rine to roote,
340 Venus her husband hath not such a foote.

   Dor. O thou whose cheeks are like the skye so blewe,
Whose nose is rubye, of the sunnlike hue,
Whose forhead is most plaine without all rinkle,

Whose eyes like starrs in frosty night doe twinkle,
Most hollowe are thy eyelidds, & thy ball
Whiter then ivory, brighter yea withall,
Whose ledge of teeth is farre more bright then jett is,
Whose lipps are too, too good for any lettice,
O doe thou condiscend vnto my boone,
Graunt mee thy love, graunt it, O silver spoone,   350
Silver moone, silver moone.
    Cli. Graunt mee thy love, to speake I first begunne,
Graunt mee thy love, graunt it, O golden sunne.
    Nar. Nor sunne, nor moone, nor twinkling starre in
        skye,
Nor god, nor goddesse, nor yet nimphe am I,
And though my sweete face bee sett out with rubye,
You misse your marke, I am a man as you bee.
    Dor. A man, Narcisse, thou hast a manlike figure ;
Then bee not like vnto the savage tiger,   F. 75ʳ rev.
So cruell as the huge camelion,   360
Nor yet so changing as small elephant.
A man, Narcisse, then bee not thou a wolfe,
To devoure my hart in thy mawes griping gulfe,
Bee none of these, & lett not nature vaunt her
That shee hath made a man like to a panther ;
A man thou art, Narcisse, & soe are wee,
Then love thou vs againe as wee love thee.
    Nar. A man I am, & sweare by gods above
I cannot yett find in my heart to love.
    Dor. Cannott find love in hart! O search more narrowe, 370
Thou well shalt knowe him by his ivory arrowe ;
That arrowe, when in breast, my bloud was tunninge,
Broacht my harts barrell, sett it all a runninge,
Which with loves liquor vnles thou doe staunch,
All my lifes liquor will runne out my paunche.

Nar. Why would you have mee love? You talke most
  oddlye,
Love is a naughty thinge & an ungodlye.
  Cli. Is love ungodlye? Love is still a god.
  Nar. But in his nonage allwaies vnder rodde.
380 *Amb.* O love, Narcissus, wee beseech thee, O love.
  Nar. Noe love, good gentiles, Ile assure you, noe
  love.
    [*Exeunt* DORASTUS *et* CLINIAS, *ambulat* NARCISSUS.

        Enter FLORIDA, CLOIS.

F. 74' rev. Clois, what ist I wis that I doe see,
  What forme doth charme this storme within my breast,
  What face, what grace, what race may that same bee,
  So faire, so rare, debonaire, breeds this vnrest?
  How white, how bright, how light, like starre of Venus
  His beames & gleames so streames so faire between
  vs!
    Clo. 'Tis Venus sure, why doe wee stand and palter?
  Lett vs goe shake our thighes vpon the altar.
390 *Flo.* Most brightest Hasparus, for thou seemst to mee
  soe,
  I, and in very deed thou well maist bee soe,
  For as bigg as a man is every plannett,
  Although it seemes a farre that wee may spanne it,
  Shine thou on mee, sweet plannet, bee soe good
  As with thy fiery beames to warme my bloud;
  Ile beare thee light, and thinke light of the burthen,
  And say, light plannett neare was heavy lurden.
    Nar. To speake the truth, faire maid, if you will have
  vs,
  O Œdipus I am not, I am Davus.

14

Clo. Good Master Davis, bee not so discourteous
As not to heare a maidens plaint for vertuous.

    Nar. Speake on a Gods name, so love bee not the
        theame.

    Flo. O, whiter then a dish of clowted creame,
Speake not of love ? How can I overskippe
To speake of love to such a cherrye lippe ?

    Nar. It would beseeme a maidens slender vastitye
Never to speake of any thinge but chastitye.

    Flo. As true as Helen was to Menela F. 74ʳ rev.
So true to thee will bee thy Florida.

    Clo. As was to trusty Pyramus truest Thisbee
So true to you will ever thy sweete Clois bee.

    Flo. O doe not stay a moment nor a minute,
Loves is a puddle, I am ore shooes in it.

    Clo. Doe not delay vs halfe a minutes mountenance
That ar in love, in love with thy sweet countenance.

    Nar. Then take my dole although I deale my alms
        ill,
Narcissus cannot love with any damzell ;
Although, for most part, men to love encline all,
I will not, I, this is your answere finall.
And so farwell ; march on doggs, love's a griper,
If I love any, 'tis Tickler & Piper.
Ah, the poore rascall, never ioyd it since
His fellow iugler first was iugled hence,
Iugler the hope ; but now to hunte abraode,
Where, if I meete loves little minitive god,
Ile pay his breech vntill I make his bumme ake,
For why, the talke of him hath turnd my stomacke.
                                 [*Exit.*

    Flo. And is hee gone ? Letts goe & dye, sweet Cloris,
For poets of our loves shall write the stories.

15

430   *Cli.* Well mett, faire Florida sweete, which way goe
you ?

F. 73ʳ rev.   *Flo.* In faith, sweete Clinias, I cannot knowe you.

    Dor. Noe, knowe, but did you see the white Narcisse ?

    Clo. The whitest man alive a huntinge is ;

Hee that doth looke farre whiter then the vilett,

Or moone at midday, or els skye at twilight.

    Cli. That is the same, even that is that Narcissus,

Hee that hath love despis'd, & scorned vs.

    Flo. Not you alone hee scornes, but vs also ;

O doe not greive when maids part stakes in woe.

440 O, that same youthe's the scummer of all skorne,

Of surquedry the very shooing horne,

Piller of pride, casting topp of contempt,

Stopple of statelines for takinge vente.

Many youthes, many maids sought him to gaine,

Noe youthes, noe maids could ever him obtaine :

Then thus I pray, & hands to heaven vpp leave,

So may hee love & neare his love atcheive.

Looke you for maids no more, our parte is done,

Wee come but to bee scornd, & so are gone.   [*Exeunt.*

450   *Dor.* But wee have more to doe, that have wee perdie,

Wee must a fish & hunt the hare so hardye,

For even as after hare runnes swiftest beagle,

So doth Narcissus our poore harts corneagle.   [*Exeunt.*

Enter ECCHO.

F. 73ʳ rev.   Who, why, wherfore, from whence or what I am,

Knowe, if you aske, that Eccho is my name,

16

That cannott speake a woord, nor halfe a sillable,
Vnles you speake before so intelligible.
But ho, the hobby horse, youle think 't absurde
That I should of my selfe once speake a woord.
'Tis true; but lett your wisdomes tell me than   460
How'de you know Eccho from another man?
I was a well toung'd nimphe, but what of that?
My mother Juno still to hold in chatte,
With tales of tubbes, from thence I ever strove,
Whiles nimphes abroad lay allwaies vnder Jove.
But oh, when drift was spied, my angry grammer
Made ever since my tottering tongue to stammer;
And now, in wild woods, & in moist mountaines,
In high, tall valleys, & in steepye plaines,
Eccho I live, Eccho, surnam'd the dolefull,   470
That, in remembrance, now could weepe a bowlfull;
Or rather, if you will, Eccho the sorrowfull,
That, in remembrance, now could weepe a barrowfull.
(Within.   Yolp! yolpe!)   [*Exit clamans Yolpe!*

Enter DORASTUS, NARCISSUS, CLINIAS.

Cantantes.

Harke, they crye, I heare by that
The doggs have putt the hare from quatte,
Then woe bee vnto little Watt,   F. 72ᵛ rev.
   Yolp, yolp, yolp, yolp!

Hollowe in the hind doggs, hollowe,
So come on then, solla, solla,
And lett vs so blithly followe,   480
   Yolp, &c.

O, the doggs ar out of sight,
But the crye is my delight;
Harke how Jumball hitts it right,
   Yolp, &c.

Over briars, over bushes;
Whose affeard of pricks & pushes,
Hee's no hunter woorth two rushes,
   Yolp, &c.

490   But how long thus shall wee wander?
O, the hares a lusty stander,
Follow apace, the doggs are yonder,
   Yolp, &c.   *[Exeunt.*

Enter one with a buckett and boughes and grasse.

A well there was withouten mudd,
Of silver hue, with waters cleare,
Whome neither sheepe that chawe the cudd,
Shepheards nor goates came ever neare;
Whome, truth to say, nor beast nor bird,
Nor windfalls yet from trees had stirrde.
          [He strawes the grasse about the buckett.

F. 72ʳ. rev. And round about it there was grasse,
   500   As learned lines of poets showe,
Which by next water nourisht was;   *[Sprinkle water.*
Neere to it too a wood did growe, *[Sets down the bowes.*
To keep the place, as well I wott,
With too much sunne from being hott.
And thus least you should have mistooke it,
The truth of all I to you tell:
Suppose you the well had a buckett,
And so the buckett stands for the well;

18

And 'tis, least you should counte mee for a sot O,   510
A very pretty figure cald *pars pro toto*.   [*Exit.*

Enter Dorastus, Eccho *answeringe him within.*

Dor. Narcissus ?
  Ecc. Kisse us.
Kisse you ; who are you, with a botts take you ?
      Botts take you.
Botts take mee, you rogue ?
      You rogue.
Slidd, hee retortes woord for woord.
      Woord for woord.
Clinias, prethy, where art thou, Clinias ?   520
      In, yee asse.
In where—in a ditch ?
      Itch.
What is his businesse ?   F. 71ʳ rev.
      At his businesse.
You don't tell mee trulye.
      You lye.
Say so againe, ile cudgell you duely.
      You doe lye.
Of your tearmes you are very full.   530
      Your a very foole.
Doe you crowe, I shall cracke your coxcombe.
      Coxcombe.
I shall make you whine & blubber.
      Lubber.
Youle make an end & dispatch.
      Patch.
Goe to, youle let these woordes passe.
      Asse.

19

540 If I come to you Ile make you singe a palinodye.
        Noddye.
Foole, coxcombe, lubber, patch, & noddye,
Are these good woords to give a bodye ?
Doe not provoke me, I shall come.
        Come.
Meete mee if you dare.
        If you dare.
I come, despaire not.
        Spare not.   [*Exit.*

F. 71ʳ rev.

        Enter CLINIAS, ECCHO *answeringe within.*

550 *Cli.* Dorastus, where art thou, Dorastus ?
    Ecc. Asse to vs.
Asse to you, whose that's an asse to you ?
        You.
Know mee for what I am, as good as your selfe.
        Elfe.
Elfe ! Why I hope you ben't so malaparte.
        All a parte.
All apart, yes, wee ar alone ; but you doe not meane to
    fight, I trust in Jove ?
560   Trust in Jove.
Jove helpes then if wee fight, but wee trust to our
    swoordes.
        Woordes.
Woordes ; why, doe you thinke tis your woordes shall vs
    affright ?
        Right.
'Tis noe such matter, you are mightely out.
        Loute.

20

Lout, dost abuse mee so ? Goe to, y'are a scall scabbe.
 Rascall scabbe. 570
Rascall scabbe, why thou groome base & needye !
 Niddye.
Slidd, if I meete you Ile bange you.
 Hange you.
Ist so ; nay then, Ile bee at hand, kee pickpurse. F. 70ʳ rev.
 Pickpurse.
Dare you vse mee thus to my face, spidar ?
 I dare.
But will you stand too't & not flintch ?
 Not flinch. 580
Well, meete mee, I am like iron & steele, trustye.
 Rustye.
Rusty, what, mocke mee to my face againe ?
 Asse againe.
Out of dowbt, if wee meete I shall thee boxe.
 Oxe.
Why, the foole rides mee, I am spurrgald & iolted.
 Jolthead.
Jolthead ! this is more then I can brooke.
 Rooke. 590
Rooke too, nay then, as farr as a knockinge goes
 I am yours to commaund, sir.
 Come on, sir. [*Exit.*

Enter NARCISSUS.

O, I am weary ; I have runne to daye
Ten miles, nay, 10 & a quarter I dare saye.
You may beleeve it, for my ioyntes are numme,
And every finger truly is a thumbe.

21

For my younge hunters, Clinias & Dorastus,

Surely so farre to day they have out past vs,

600 That heere I am encompast round about,
And doe not knowe the way nor in nor out.
What Holla, holla!
        Ecc. Holla, holla.
Is any body nye?
                I.
Come neere.
                Come neere.
Whither?
                Hither.

610 I prethy helpe mee foorth, els I am the rude woods
        forfeiture.
                Faire feature.
O lord, sir, tis but your pleasure to call it soe.
                Its soe.
I had rather have your counsell how to gett out of this
        laborinthe.
                Labour in't.
Labour in't, why soe I doe, sore against my will, but to
        labour out of it what shall I doe?

620   Doe.
Nay, pray helpe mee out if you love mee.
                Love mee.
Come neere, then, why doe you flye?
                Why doe you flye?
Where b'ye?

Heerbye.
Let vs come together.
                Let vs come together.
I prethy come.

630   I come.

22

Let mee dye first ere thou meddle with mee.
      Meddle with mee.   *[Exit.*

Enter Dorastus, Clinias, *at 2 doores.*

Cli. Wast you, Dorastus, mockt mee all this season ?
Dor. Pray, Clinias, hold your tounge, y'haue little
    reason
To make a foole of mee & mocke mee too.
Cli. Nay, sir, twas you that mockt mee, so you doe ;
While heere I cald for you by greenwood side,
You gibde on mee, which you shall deare abide.
Dor. Nay, you did call mee, that I was loath to heare,
Truly such woords as a dogg would not beare.   640
But as I scorne so to bee ast & knaved,
Soe truly doe I scorne to bee outbraved.
Cli. O frieng panne of all fritters of fraud,
My scindifer, that longe hath beene vndrawde,
Shall come out of his sheath most fiery hott,
And slice thee small, even as hearbes to pott.
Dor. Thou huge & humminge humblebee, thou hornett,
Come doe thy worst, I say that I doe scorne it.
Cli. O with thy bloud Ile make so redd my whineard,
As ripest liquor is of grapes in vineyearde.   F. 69ʳ rev.
Dor. And with thy bloud Ile make my swoord so   650
    ruddye,
As skye at eventide shall not bee soe bloudye.
                    [They fight & fall.
Cli. O, O, about my harte I feele a paine ;
Dorastus, hold thy handes, for I am slaine.
Dor. This shall thy comfort bee when thou art dead,
That thou hast kild mee too, for I am spedd.

Cli. O, I am dead, depart life out of hand,
Stray, soule, from home vnto the Stingian strand.
    Dor. Goe thou, my ghost, complaine thee vnto Rha-
    damant

660 That the 3 sisters hartes are made of adamant.
    Cli. Since wee must passe ore lake in Charons ferry,
Had wee Narcissus wee should bee more merrye.
    Dor. My soule doth say that wee must goe before,
Narcisse will overtake vs at the shore ;
And that that mockt vs both, deformed dwarfe,
Will er't bee long arive at Charons wharfe.
    Cli. Lett us, Dorastus, die, departe, decease ;
Wee lovd in strife, & lett vs dye in peace.
    Dor. Stay, take mee with you, letts togither goe.

670   *Am.* Vild world adieu, wee die, ô ô ô ô!

Enter NARCISSUS.

Does the hagg followe ? Stay for her never durst I ;
Sh'as made mee runne so longe that I am thurstye,
F. 68ʳ rev. But O, yee gods immortall, by good fortune
Heere is a well in good time & oportune ;
Drinke, drinke, Narcissus, till thy belly burst,
Water is Rennish wine to them that thirst.
But oh remaine & let thy christall lippe
Noe more of this same cherrye water sippe ;
What deadly beautye or what aerye nimphe

680 Is heare belowe now seated in the limphe ?
Looke, looke, Narcissus, how his eyes are silver,
Looke, least those eyes thy hart from thee doe pilfer,
Yet O looke not, for by these eyes so headye,
Thy hart from thee is filcht away allreadye ;

24.

O Well, how oft I kisse thy wholsome liquor,
While on my love kisses I heape a dicker.
O love, come foorth accordinge to my mind,
How deepe I dive yet thee I cannott find ;
O love, come foorth, my face is not so foule
That thou shouldst scorne mee ; pittye mee, poor soule.   690
Well, dost thou scorne mee ?   Nimphes they did not
     soe,
They had a better thought of mee I trowe.
Not care of Ceres, Morpheus, nor of Bacchus,
That is meate, drinke, & sleepe from hence shall take vs ;
Heere will I dye, this well shall bee my tombe,
My webb is spunne ; Lachesis, loppe thy loome.
                        [Lye downe & rise vpp againe. F. 68ʳ rev.
Tell mee, you woods, tell mee, you oakes soe stronge,
Whether in all your life, your life so longe,
So faire a youth pinde thus, & tell mee trulye
Whether that any man ere lov'd so cruellye.   700
The thinge I like I see, but what I see
And like, natheles I cannot find perdie,
And that that greives my liver most, no seas
Surging, mountaines, monstrous or weary ways,
Nor walls with gates yshutt doe mee remove ;
A little water keepes mee from my love.
Come out, come out, deare boye.
  Ecc. Come out, deare boye.
  [*Nar.*] Thy frend I am, O doe not mee destroye ;
Thou dost putt out thy hand as I doe mine,   710
And thou dost pinke vpon mee with thine eyen,
Smile as I smile ; besides I tooke good keepe,
And saw thee eke shedd teares when I did weepe,
And by thy lippes moving, well I doe suppose
Woordes thou dost speake, may well come to our nose ;

For to oure cares I am sure they never passe,
Which makes me to crye out, alas!
 Ecc. Alas!
 [*Nar.*] O delicate pretty youth,
720   Pretty youth;
Take on my woes pitty, youthe!
   Pittye, youthe!

F. 67ʳ rev. O sweetest boy, pray love mee!
   Pray love mee!
Or els I dye for thee,
   I dye for thee!
 [*Nar.*] Colour is gone & bloud in face is thinne,
And I am naught left now but bone & skinne;
I dye; but though I dye it shall come to passe,
730 Certes it shall, that I which whilome was
The flower of youth, shalbee made flower againe.
I dye; farewell, O boy belov'd in vaine.
 [*Ecc.*] O boy belov'd in vaine.
        [NARCISSUS *risinge vp againe.*
And so I died & sunke into my grandam,
Surnamde old earth: lett not your iudgments randome,
For if you take mee for Narcissus y'are very sillye,
I desire you to take mee for a daffa downe dillye;
For so I rose, & so I am in trothe,
As may appeare by the flower in my mouthe.
740 *Ecc.* Now auditors of intelligence quicke,
I pray you suppose that Eccho is sicke;
Sicke at the hart, for you must thinke,
For lacke of love shee could nor eate nor drinke;
Soe that of her nothinge remainde but bone,
And that they say was turn'd into a stone.

F. 67ʳ rev. Onely her voice was left, as by good happe
You may perceive if you imparte a clappe.   [*Exit.*

26

Enter the Porter *as Epilogue.*

Are those the ladds that would doe the deede?
They may bee gone, & God bee their speede;
Ile take vpp their buckett, but I sweare by the water,   750
I have seene a farre better play at the theater.
Ile shutt them out of doores, 'tis no matter for their
        larges;
Thinke you well of my service, & Ile beare the charges.
If there bee any that expecte some dances,
'Tis I must perform it, for my name is Frances.

FINIS.

27

APPENDIX.

I.

F. 84' rev. *A speech made for the foresaid porter, who pronounc't it in the hall before most of the house and Master Præsident, that had sconc't him* 10 *groates for letting the fidlers into the hall at Christmas.*

Ille ego qui quondam, I am hee that in ould season have made Lilly leape out of his skinne, & with a muster of sentences out of his syntaxis have besieged the eares of the audience in the behalfe of the wretched. But alas!—Mihi isthic nec seritur nec metitur; it is to mee neither a sorrye turne nor a merrye turne. I have sifted out for other mens sakes the flower of my fancye, that I have left nothing but the branne in my braine. And yet who is there amongst them that in the depth of
10 my distresse will speake for the poore porter, who meltes the muses into mourninge or turnes Parnassus into plaintes, Hellicon into heavines, Apollo into an apollogie, for my sake? My learninge goeth not beyond Lillye, nor my reading beyond my rules, yet have I for them so canvast their concavitye that I have opened their entraills, so dived into the depth of them that I have manifested their marrowe, soe pried into their profunditye that I have plac't the verye pith of them before you. And, alas that I should
F. 83' rev. now speake for my selfe, what remaines for mee but the
20 rinde & the barke, when I have given the roote &

28

the bodye to others? What remaines for mee but the shell, when I have given others the substaunce, what remaines for mee but the curdes, when I have given others the creame? Yea, what is left for mee but the paringes, when I have given others the peares? But I therin made knowen my valour, for you knowe, Aliorum vitia cernere oblivisci suorum, to supplye other mens wants & to forgett his owne, proprium est stultitiæ, is the parte of a stoute man; since then I must speake for my selfe, Stat mihi casus renovare omnes; you shall 30 heare the whole cause, case, and the course of it.

Sub nocte silenti, (i) in nocte vel paulo ante noctem, cum spectatur in ignibus aurum; when you might have seene gold in the fier, the fier shin'de so like gold, Ecce per opaca locorum, came the fidlers creeping alonge, densa subter testudine casus, their instruments vnder their arms, in their cases, & at lenghe, Itum est in viscera terræ, broke open into the harte of the hall; neither when they were there could they bee content to warme their fingers by the fier and bee gone, though I 40 would have persuaded them thereto, but Iuvat vsque morari et conferre gradum; they would needes staye & the youth daunce; but oh to see, woe to see, that pleasure is but a pinch and felicitye but a phillippe; when as Juvat ire per altum, some were cutting capers aloft in the ayre, canit similiter huic, and they likewise with their minstrelsey fitting it to their footing, all on a sud- daine, Subito I may say to them, but Repente to mee, their sporte was spoild, their musicke marrd, their daun- cinge dasht with a vox hominem sonat, with a voyce, 50 with an awefull voice, Hæccine fieri flagitia; ar these the fruites of the fires; statur a me, (i) sto, statur ab illis, (i) stant; they that even now scrap't so fast with their

29

stickes fell now to scraping faster with their leggs; their
fum fum was turn'd to mum mum, and their pleasaunt
melodye to most pittifull making of faces; but when they
look't that their fiddles should have flyen about their
eares, their calveskin cases about their calveshead pates,
as the sunne shines brightest through a shower, so did
60 softnes in the midst of severitye: there was noe more
F. 82' rev. said to them but, Teque his ait eripe flammis; they were
best, since they had made many mens heeles warme with
shakinge, to coole their owne by quaking without doore.
But the more mercy was shewed before, the lesse was
left for mee. Had I beene dealt with soe mercifullye, I
had not neede to have come with this exclamation, or
had it beene but gratia ab officio, but a groat out of mine
office, I should not have stonied the stones nor rented
the rockes with my dolorous outcryes.
70 But when it shall come to denarii dicti quod denos,
when tenn groats shall make a muster togeather and sitte
heavy on my head, actum est ilicet, the porter periit. O
weathercoke of wretchednes that I am, seated on the
may-pole of misfortune; whither shall I turne, or to
whome shall I looke for releife ? Shall I speake to my
minstrells for my money ? Why, they have allready
forsaken mee, to the verifieng of the ould proverbe;
Quantum quisque sua nummorum servat in arcā, tantum
habet et fidei ; as long as a man hath money in his purse,
80 so long hee shall have the fidlers. What is to bee looked
for of them that will doe nothing without pay, and hard-
mony for their harmonye ? Shall I speake to my frends ?
Why : nullus ad amissas ibit amicus opes. Oh, then, lett
F. 43'. rev. mee runne to the speare of Achilles (recorded by auncient
philosophers) which first hurt mee and last can heale
mee : lett my penitencye find pittye, and my confession

30

move compassion; if you will live according to rule, ever after penitet, tædet, lett miseret, miserescit succeede.

That they came in, it was a fault of oversight in not overseeing my office : if any should slinke by Cerberus 90 out of hell, it weare a thing to bee wondred at, & yet wee see there doth, ther are so many spirritts walking. If any should steale by Janus into heaven, it weare much woorthy of marvaile, and yet wee see there doth, there are soe many of Jupiters lemmans : if anye should skippe in or out by mee it is not to bee admired : for why? Cerberus the porter of hell hath 3 heads, Janus hath two, & I your poore colledg porter have but one.   That they weare not putt out of the colledge when they weare in, it was a fault; but a fault of curtesie ; for who could 100 find in his hart, when hee seeth a man accompanied with musicke, musis comitantibus, to bidd him, Ibis Homere foras, gett you home for an asse ?

But though my breast (I must confesse) weare then somewhat moved with their melodye, yet heerafter my breast shall bee marble when they warble : Nemo sibi Mimos accipere debet favori, I will never lett in minstrells againe vpon favour; for your selves I can say no more but profit; & when (after this Christmas cheere is ended) you fall againe to your studdies, I could wish that 110 Hippocrene may bee Hippocrise, the muses Muskadine, & the Pierides pies every day for your sakes; and as for my tenn groates, if it will please you to remitte it, I will give you decies decem mille gratiarum.   Dixi.

31

II.

A speech delivered by Francis Clarke to the Ladie Keneda.

Noble ladye, give him leave that hath beene so bolde
as to take leave, to speake before your ladyshipp, and
out of the prognosticks, not of profound pond or deepe
dale, but out of the candlesticke of mine owne observation,
to give your ladyshipp some lightning of a great thunder
that will happen in the morning.

The reason of it is a flatt, slimye, & sulphureous
matter exhaled out of the kitchins & enflamed in the
highest region of the dripping pannes, which will breed
10 fiery commetts with much lightning and thunder. And
the influence of it will so domineere in the cooks heads,
that are brought vpp under the torridd zone of the chimney,
that few of them will take rest this night, & suffer as
few to take rest in the morning. They have sett a little
porch before so great an house, and have called their show
the flye. Some say because a maide comming to towne
with butter was mett by a cooke & by him deceaved in a
wood neare adioyning, whose laments the dryades and
hamadriades of the place, pittieng, turned her into a
20 butterflie; & ever since the cooks are bound to this
anniversary celebration of her metamorphosis; but soft,
if the cooks heare that the porridgpott of my mouth
F. 45ᵛ rev. runnes over soe, they will keele it with the ladle of
reprehension; therfore I will make hast away, onely asking
this boone, which wilbee as good as a bone to the cookes;
that your ladyshipps servaunt Monsieur Piers may ride to-
morrowe with the fierye fraternitye of his fellowe cookes,

32

& make vpp the worthy companye of the round table, which they are resolvd not to leave till the whole house goe rounde with them.

III.

A Speech spoken by Francis Clarke in the behalfe of the freshmen.

Ne sævi, magne sacerdos, bee not so severe, great session holder; lett pittie prevaile over the pœnitent, lett thy woords of woormwood goe downe againe into thy throate, & so by consequence into thy belly, but lett not those goe to the place from whence they came, & so by cohærence to the place of exequution : and though these bee, as it is rightly said in the rule, Turba gravis paci placidæque inimica quieti, yet thinke what goes next before, Sis bonus ô felixque tuis : and although I must needes say I am sorry for it that Fertur atrocia flagitia 10 designasse, yet remember what followes immediatlye in the place ; Teque ferunt iræ pœnituisse tuæ.

Your lordshipp is learned as well as I (it is bootles & I should offer you the bootes), you knowing the Latine to expounde.

I am heere the jaylor, the Janus, the janitor; you are the judge, the justice, the Jupiter, to this miserable companye ; yet beare I not two faces under a hoode, neither deale I doubly betweene your lordshipp & the lewde ; for though Janus & the jaylor goe together, vt bifrons, 20 custos, yet Bos stands for a barre to distinguish the jaylor from the theefe, vt bifrons, custos, bos, fur.

O that you weare Jupiter, to bee a helping father to these sonnes of sorrow, or I weare Janus indeed, that I might have two tongues to intreate for this pittifull crew.

Looke, O thou flower of favour, thou marigold of mercye
and columbine of compassion, looke, O looke on the
dolorous dew dropps distilld from the limbecks or loope-
holes of their eyes, and plentifully powred on the flower
30 of their faces ; O see in these (O thou most exalted
eldest sonne of Justice) a lamentable example ; consider
that homo bulla, honor is but a blast ; pittie, O pitty the
cause of these hopeles, helples, hartles and indeed half-
hanged young men ; if they have erred, humanum est,
they are men ; looke not thou for that of them which you
can but expect of gods. Have they spoken against the
lawes of your court, why, Dolet dictum imprudenti
adolescenti et libero : has their tongue tript, why, Lingua
percurrit, it was too quicke for the witt, quicknes is
40 commendable. Pectora percussit, have they fought with
your ·highnes servaunts, have they beene obstinate ?
Why, they have had their punishment, and toties quoties,
went either wett skind or dry beaten to bedd. Quid
est quod, in hac causā defensionis egeat ; take pittie (O
thou peerles patterne of equity) if on nothing els, yet on
their youth.

Some of them are heires, all of good abilitye ; I beseech your lordshipp with the rest of the ioynd stooles, I
would say the bench, take my foolish iudgment, & lett
50 them fine for it, merce them according to their merritts
and their purses, wee shall all fare the better for it.

As for other punishments (I speake it with weeping
teares) they have suffered no small affliction in my
keeping ; Est locus in carcere quod dungeanum appella-
tur ; there they lay, noctes atque dies, at no great charge,
for, Constat parvo fames ; but so laded with irons that I
made them Livida armis brachia, & now, see, they are
come foorth after all, Trepidus morte futura.

O miseresce malis, take pitty on the poore prisners, Patres æquum esse censent nos iam iam; you may very 60 well remember, since yourselfe weare in the same case. Cutt not off for some few slippes those younge plantes of such towardnes; make not mothers weepe, winke at small faultes, rovoke your sentence, lett the common good have their fines, mee have my fees, they have their lives, and all shalbee well pleased. Dixi.

IV.

A letter composd for Franckė Clarke, the porter of S. John's, F. 84ᵛ rev. *who in his brother's behalfe did breake one's head with a blacke staffe.*

To Master Laude, then Proctor.

Worshipfull and woorthy Master Proctor, wheras I, your poore vassaile, in charitye towardes my afflicted brother, have stepped over the shooes of my duetye in participatinge or accommodatinge my blacke staffe to the easinge of his over-charged artickles & members, wherby I have iustlye plucked the oulde house, or rather the maine beame of your indignation, upon my impotent and impudent shoulders, I doe now beseech you upon the knees of my sorrowfullnes and marybones of repentance to forgive mee all delictes & crimes as have beene 10 formerly committed.

And wheras you, contrary to my desertes, have out of the bottomles pitt of your liberalitye restored mee out of the porters lodge of miserye into the tower of fœlicitie, by giving that which was due from mee (silly mee) vnto your worshippfull selfe, I meane my ladye pecunia; lett mee intreate you that I may burden the leggs of your

liberalitie so much farther, as to deliver mee the afore-
said blacke staffe, without which I am a man & noe
20 beast, a wretch & no porter. But wheras it is thus
by my most vnfortunate fate, that so woorthy a President

hath seene so vnworthy a present, I cannott but condole
my tragedies, committing you to the profunditye or
abisse of your liberalitie, & my selfe to the 3 craues of
my adversitie. Dixi.

NOTES TO THE PLAY OF "NARCISSUS."

NOTES TO THE PLAY OF "NARCISSUS."

Line 1. *Master and Mistris.*—Doubtless the President of
S. John's and his wife. The office was held at this time by
Ralph Hutchinson, who had been elected to it in 1590, after
holding for some years the college living of Charlbury, Oxon.
Little seems to be known of Mrs. Hutchinson beyond the fact
that after her husband's death in 1606 she placed his effigy in
the college chapel.

Line 39. *Rebateth.*—To rebate, to blunt or disedge; see
Measure for Measure, i. 4, 60—"Doth rebate and blunt his
natural edge."

Line 55. *Quaffe.*—The substantival use of this word is not
uncommon in contemporary writings. Cf., in 1579, L. Tomson,
Calvin's *Sermons on Timothy, &c.*, p. 512, col. 2: "Now they
thinke that a sermon costeth no more then a quaffe wil them."

Line 78. *Ladds of mettall.*—Cf. 1 *Henry IV.* ii. 4, 13.

Line 80. *No vertue extant.*—Cf. 1 *Henry IV.* ii. 4, 132, where
virtue = bravery, physical courage. The porter's use of the
phrase sounds like a quotation.

Line 97. *A the stampe.*—Halliwell gives "Stamp, a tune,"
and quotes from MS. Fairfax, 16, "Songes, stampes, and eke
daunces." Cf. also *Midsummer Night's Dream*, iii. 2, 25.

Line 98. *Windsuckers.*—This old name for the kestrel, or
wind-hover, is of tolerably frequent occurrence. It is used
metaphorically of a person ready to pounce on anything. "There
is a certain envious windsucker that hovers up and down"
(Chapman).

Line 101. *I pre, sequor.*—Literally, "Go before, I follow." The
porter supplies a free translation in the words "one of your

39

consorte." Cf. the use of the phrase "to be hail-fellow-well-met with anyone."

Line 109. *Condolent* here means *expressing sorrow.* For this sense see Wood, Ath. Oxon. (R)—"His vein for ditty and amorous ode was deemed most lofty, condolent, and passionate."

Line 110. *Suffocat.*—The porter's substitute for *sufficit;* though, strictly speaking, the *o* should be long.

Line 111. *I tickle them for a good voice.*—Besides the ordinary metaphorical meaning of to flatter, *tickle* sometimes = to serve one right, to make one pay for a thing. For this sense see 1 *Henry IV.* ii. 4, 489, "I'll tickle ye for a young prince, i' faith;" and cf. *Ibid.* ii. 1, 66. Probably the expression has a similar force here.

Line 114. *Butterd beare.*—Ale boiled with lump-sugar, butter, and spice.

Line 122. *Act in conye.*—The adjective *incony*, with the apparent sense of fine, delicate, is used twice by Costard in *Love's Labour's Lost* (iii. 136, iv. 1, 144) and also in Marlowe's *Jew of Malta*, iv. 5—"While I in thy incony lap do tumble." Other examples are rare, and I have not found any instance of an adverbial use. A second, though much less probable interpretation of the passage is suggested by the frequent use of *cony* as a term of endearment to a woman (cf. Skelton's *Eleanor Rummyng*, 225—"He called me his whytyng, his nobbes, and his conny"). If, however, "act in conye" were equivalent to "act as woman," *i.e.* take a female part, examples of analogous constructions should be forthcoming.

Line 129. *Lovely.*—Here used in the sense of loving, tender. Cf. *Taming of the Shrew*, iii. 2, 125—"And seal the title with a lovely kiss."

Line 156. *All and some.*—An expression meaning everyone, everything, altogether :

> "For which the people blisful, *al and somme,*
> So cryden " . . .
> > (CHAUCER, *Anelida and Arcite*, l. 26.)

> "Thou who wilt not love, do this ;
> Learne of me what Woman is.
> Something made of thred and thrumme ;
> A meere botch of all and some."
> > (HERRICK, *Hesperides*, i. 100.)

40

Line 160. *Cappes a thrumming.*—Cf. *Knight of the Burning Pestle*, iv. 5—

"And let it ne'er be said for shame that we, the youths of London,
Lay thrumming of our caps at home, and left our custom undone."

To *thrum* = to beat in the Suffolk dialect.

Line 167. *Shrimpe.*—This use of the word in the sense of child, offspring (or possibly as a term of endearment, "little one") is not common. It was generally employed contemptuously, and meant a dwarfish or stunted creature, as in 1 *Henry VI.* ii. 3, 23. See, however, *Love's Labour's Lost*, v. 2, 594.

Line 193. *Oddes* here = contention, quarrel. For this sense compare—

" I cannot speak
Any beginning to this peevish odds."
(*Othello*, ii. 3, 185.)

and also *Henry V.* ii. 4, 129, and *Timon of Athens*, iv. 3, 42.

Line 195. *Seven yeares I was a woman.*—The blindness of Tiresias is most frequently ascribed, either to his having, when a child, revealed the secrets of the gods, or to his having gazed upon Athenè bathing, on which occasion the goddess is said to have deprived him of sight. Another tradition, however (adhered to by Ovid, *Met.* iii. 516, etc.), relates that Tiresias beheld two serpents together ; he struck at them, and, happening to kill the female, was himself changed into a woman. Seven years later he again encountered two serpents, but now killed the male, and resumed the shape of man. Zeus and Hera, disputing over the relative happiness of man and woman, referred the matter to Tiresias, as having a practical knowledge of both conditions. He favoured Zeus's assertion that a woman possessed the more enjoyments ; whereupon Hera, indignant, blinded him, while Zeus bestowed on him, in compensation, the power of prophecy.

Line 197. *Fold.*—The omission of a prefix to suit the exigencies of metre, common enough in verbs such as defend, defile, becomes remarkable when the force of the prefix itself is such as to change entirely the meaning of the verb. Examples of omission in such cases are comparatively rare, but they are not confined to our own language. See Vergil, *Aen.* i. 262—

" Longius et volvens fatorum arcana movebo "—

and cf. also *Aen.* v. 26, and Cicero's *Brutus*, 87.

Line 223. *Catch audacitye.*—For the old metaphorical use of catch cf. Wyclif's Bible (1 Tim. vi. 12), "Catche euerlastyng lyf."

Line 227. *Curromanstike*, chiromantic, *i.e.* pertaining to chiromancy ; the rhyme being probably responsible for the use of the adjective rather than the noun.

Line 229. *The table*, etc.—" The table-line, or line of fortune, begins under the mount of Mercury, and ends near the index and middle finger. . . . When lines come from the mount of Venus, and cut the line of life, it denotes the party unfortunate in love and business, and threatens him with some suddain death " (*The True Fortune-teller*, or *Guide to Knowledge*, 1686).

Line 236. *Sheppbiter.*—A malicious, surly fellow ; according to Dyce, "a cant term for a thief." See *Twelfth Night*, ii. 5, 6, " The niggardly, rascally sheep-biter."

Line 246. *What.*—MS. has the abbreviation wth, usually denoting *with*, but evidently substituted here, by a copyist's error, for w^t = *what*.

Line 247. *They can but bring*, etc.—W. Carew Hazlitt (*English Proverbs*, p. 28) quotes from Heywood, 1562—" A man maie well bring a horse to the water, but he can not make him drinke without he will." He also mentions that the proverb is ascribed (probably falsely) to Queen Elizabeth, in the *Philosopher's Banquet* (1614).

Line 261. *I* = ay.—Both spellings occur in the MS. For the common use of the capital *I* in this sense, see Juliet's play upon the word—

> " Hath Romeo slain himself? Say thou but ' I,'
> And that bare vowel ' I ' shall poison more
> Than the death-darting eye of cockatrice ;
> I am not I, if there be such an I."
> (*Romeo and Juliet*, iii. 2, 45, etc.)

Line 262. *In spight of . . . pye.*—Alluding to the common belief in the pie, or magpie, as a bird of ill-omen.

Line 266. *Phibbus.*—The same spelling as in *Midsummer Night's Dream*, i. 2, 37.

Line 270. *Baskett dagger.*—Doubtless a weapon resembling the basket-*sword*, which had a hilt specially designed to protect the hand from injury. Cf. *2 Henry IV*. ii. 4, 141.

Line 275. *Footinge*, step, tread ; cf. *Merchant of Venice*, v. 24.

Line 279.—*Late-mouse.*—A facetious spelling of Latmus, the "mount of oblivion."

Line 281. *Shift* originally meant simply change, substitution of one thing for another. Cf. *Timon of Athens*, i. 1, 84— "Fortune, in her shift and change of mood." Wotton writes— "My going to Oxford was not merely for shift of air." From this arose the later sense of a change of clothing, in which the word is here used; and which has now become further limited, *shift* amongst the lower classes being equivalent to an undergarment.

Line 282. *Cantle.*—A corner, angle, small point. Cf. 1 *Henry IV.* iii. 1, 100; *Antony and Cleopatra*, iii. 10, 6. See also under *cantle* in N. E. D.

Line 283. *Portmantle.*—The older and commoner form of *portmanteau*, occurring, for example, in Howell's *Familiar Letters* (1623). Early instances of *portmanteau* are, however, to be found.

Line 296. *Ile bee a diar, etc.*—The joke is on the double meaning of *diar*; there seems to be no special significance in the choice of the colour orange-tawny.

Line 300. *Codshead* = stupid-head, foolish fellow. Cf. in 1607, Drewill's *Arraignm.* in Harl. Misc. (Malh.) iii. 56 :—"Lloyd (threatning he) woulde trye acquaintance with the other codsheade." Also, in 1594, Carew Huarte's *Exam. Wits*, i. (1596), 2 :—"His (Cicero's) sonne . . . prooued but a cods-head."

Line 301. *O eyes, noe eyes.*—The common tag from Hieronymo, in Kyd's *Spanish Tragedy*, Act iii. :

"O eyes ! No eyes, but fountains fraught with tears ;
O life ! No life, but lively form of death."

The line was a frequent subject of ridicule amongst contemporary writers; cf. *Every Man in his Humour*, i. 5, 58, etc.

Line 316. *Fennell.*—Fœniculum vulgare, considered as an inflammatory herb, and used as an emblem of flattery. Cf. *Hamlet*, iv. 5, 180.

Line 320. *Thou.*—MS. has *though.*

Line 327. *Weasand.*—This word is generally used as a noun, and itself means wind-pipe. Cf. *Tempest*, iii. 2, 99.

Line 328. *Thy face more faire, etc.*—According to some legends, Gorgon or Medusa was a beautiful maiden before Athenè, in

43

anger, changed her hair into serpents, thereby rendering her so hideous that all who saw her became petrified. Possibly, however, the allusion here is merely facetious.

Line 329. *Dishevells.*—Spreads in disorder (an intransitive use). "Their hair, curling, dishevels about their shoulders." (Sir T. Herbert.)

Line 330. *Queene of devills.*—Probably Persephone, the wife of Pluto, who ruled amongst the shades of the departed.

Line 332. *Mavors* or *Mavers* is the form from which *Mars* is contracted.

Line 337. *Silenus for streight backe.*—Silenus is usually depicted as a fat, jovial old man, intoxicated and requiring support. The comparison is of course ironical.

Line 339. *Rine* = rind or bark. The O. E. form was rinde ; but for a similar omission of *d* in the literary language cf. *lime* (O. E. linde) and *lawn* (M. E. launde).

Line 342. *Whose nose, etc.*—Cf. *Midsummer Night's Dream*, v. 338. A similar jest occurs in Peele's "Old Wives' Tale" : " Her corall lippes, her crimson chinne."

Line 345. *Thy.*—MS. has *they.*

Line 360. *Cruell, huge,* are the epithets properly belonging to *elephant ; changing, small,* to *chameleon.* See Introduction.

Line 396. *Ile beare thee light.*—If this expression be an idiom, I can find no other instance of it ; cf., however, the analogous phrase "to bear hard," *i.e.* to take ill (*Julius Cæsar*, ii. 1, 215 ; 1 *Henry IV.* i. 3, 270). The punning character of the passage makes it difficult to determine what exact meaning Florida wishes to convey. A not improbable sense would be obtained by supplying a comma after *thee*, and thus turning *light* into a nominative of address.

Line 397. *Lurden*, a clown, sluggard, ill-bred person (Halliwell).

> "And seyde, lurden, what doyst thou here ?
> Thou art a thefe, or thefys fere."
> (*MS. Cantab*, Ff. ii. 38, f. 240.)

The word occurs in *Piers Plowman.*

Line 399. *O Œdipus I am not, I am Davus.*—A quotation from Terence, *Andria*, i. 2, 23 : " Davus sum, non Œdipus."

Line 400. *Master Davis.*—Evidently an intentional anglicizing of the classical name.

44

Line 406. *Vastitye.*—So MS., possibly for *vastilye.*

Line 408. *As true as Helen, etc.*—Cf. the professions of Pyramus and Thisbe (where, however, no irony is intended), *Midsummer Night's Dream,* v. 1, 200-203.

Line 413. *Loves.*—So MS. for *love.*

Line 413. *I am ore shooes in it.*—Cf. *Two Gentlemen of Verona,* i. 1, 23 :

> " That's a deep story of a deeper love,
> For he was more than over shoes in love."

Line 414. *Mountenance,* quantity, amount. The translation of the *Romaunt of the Rose,* attributed to Chaucer, has—"The mountenance of two fynger hight."

Line 422. *Never ioyd it since.*—Cf. 1 *Henry IV.* ii. 1, 13 : " Poor fellow, never joyed since the price of oats rose ; it was the death of him."

Line 426. *Pay* = beat (still used dialectically) :

> " They with a foxe tale him soundly did pay."
> (*The King and a poore Northerne Man,* 1640.)

Line 440. *Scummer.*—The meanings of this word appear to be either various or obscure. Halliwell gives " *Scummer,* wonder ; Somerset." In Elworthy's *West Somersetshire Wordbook* the definitions stand thus : (1) row, disturbance ; (2) confusion, upset ; (3) mess, dirty muddle. Wright, in his *Provincial Dictionary,* gives the meaning as ordure, without referring the word to any special locality. Obviously, this *scummer* is not to be confounded with M. E. *scumer,* a rover or pirate.

Line 441. *Surquedry,* presumption, arrogance, conceit. Chaucer has—"Presumpcion is he whan a man taketh an emprise that him ought not to do, or ellis he may it not do & that is called surquidrie " (*Parson's Tale,* Corpus MS.).

Line 441. *Shooing-horne.*—Metaphorically, anything which helps to draw something else on : a tool. Cf. *Troilus and Cressida,* v. 1, 61 : " A thrifty shoeing-horn in a chain, hanging at his brother's leg." The expression "shoeing horn of surquedry " is thus equivalent to " chosen implement of personified arrogance."

Line 442. *Casting topp,* a peg-top. See W. Coles (1657), *Adam in Eden,* 169—"The fruit is in forme like a casting-top."

45

Line 443. *Stopple.*—The older form of stopper. Cotgrave has —" Tampon, a bung or stopple."

Line 446. *Vpp leave.*—So MS. for *vpp heave*, possibly by confusion with *vpp lift.*

Line 453. *Corneagle.*—I can find no instances whatever of this very puzzling word ; neither does it seem to be closely analogous to any known form. Can *corneagle* be a corrupt spelling of *co-niggle*, to niggle both (our hearts) together ? *Niggle* was used formerly for deceive, steal (still in the dialects), make sport of, mock; but is not, to my knowledge, compounded elsewhere with this prefix. Or is "harts corneagle " a substitution for "harts' core niggle"? (Heart's core occurs in *Hamlet.*) Both explanations have been suggested to me only as a last resource, and are too far-fetched to be at all convincing. Moreover, the context seems to require the sense of pursue, persecute, rather than of deceive.

Line 464. *Tales of tubbes.*—A characteristic rendering into Elizabethan English of Ovid's "Illa Deam longo prudens sermone tenebat." The earliest instances of the expression "tales of tubs" seem to occur about the middle of the sixteenth century. ·

Notes and Queries, series v. vol. xi. p. 505, quotes amongst "curious phrases in 1580"—"To heare some Gospel of a distaffe and tale of a tubbe" (*Beehive of the Romish Church*, fo. 275ᵇ). See also Holland's "Plutarch," p. 644, and (for further references) Dodsley-Hazlitt's *Old Plays*, ii. 335.

Line 475. *Quatte.*—A corruption of *squat*, sometimes used substantively for the sitting of a hare :

> " Procure a little sport
> And then be put to the dead quat."
> (*White Devil*, 4to, H.)

That the word in this sense was not general may be gathered from the fact that George Turberville, in his full description of the various methods of hunting the hare (*Noble Art of Venerie*, 1575), makes no use of it, but speaks constantly of the hare's form. *Quat* for *squat* (non-substantival) is still frequent in some of the dialects, and is the word specially used of a hare or other game when flattening itself on the earth to escape observation. In West Somersetshire it is used in connection with the

46

verb to go—"The hare went quat" (Elworthy). This is the modern use most nearly approximating to that of the present passage.

Line 476. *Watt*, the old name for a hare; hence metaphorically used of a wily, cautious person (Halliwell).

Line 478. *Hollowe in the hind doggs.*—Turberville, describing the hunting of hares, writes,—"One of the huntesmen shall take charge to rate & beate on *such doggs as bide plodding behinde;* and the other shall make them seeke and cast about."

Line 518. *Slidd*, God's lid, a mean oath. See *Merry Wives of Windsor*, iii. 4, 24; *Twelfth Night*, iii. 4, 427; *Every Man in his Humour*, i. 1, 56.

Line 537. *Patch.*—A term of contempt, generally supposed to have been first applied to professional fools, by reason of their parti-coloured dress. See *Tempest*, iii. 2, 71; *Comedy of Errors*, iii. 1, 32, 36.

Line 556. *Malaparte*, forward, saucy. See *Twelfth Night*, iv. 1, 47, and 3 *Henry VI.* v. 5, 32.

Line 569. *Scall scabbe.*—A scall = a scab; scald = scabby. See *Merry Wives of Windsor*, iii. 1, 123; *Twelfth Night*, ii. 5, 82; *Troilus and Cressida*, ii. 1, 31.

Line 571. *Groome.*—In M. E. this word meant simply boy, youth; hence (at a later period) serving-lad. See *Taming of the Shrew*, iii. 2, 215, and *Titus Andronicus*, iv. 2, 164.

Line 573. *Bange*, beat. Cf. *Othello*, ii. 1, 21, and *Julius Cæsar*, iii. 3, 20.

Line 575. *Kee pickpurse.*—This expression seems to be a quotation from 1 *Henry IV.* ii. 1, 53:

> "*Gads.* What, ho! Chamberlain!
> *Cham. (within).* At hand, quoth pick-purse."

I am told that the colloquial use of *kee*, or *quy*, for *quoth*, is frequent in certain parts of Scotland; but I can find no literary example of the form, and it is hard to account for its presence in this passage. The scribal substitution of *quy* for the abbreviated *quoth* might easily occur, the thorn-letter being erroneously transcribed by *y*, as in *the;* but this cannot have given rise to any M. E. phonetic change such as the spelling *kee* certainly implies.

Line 587. *Spurrgald.*—Cf. *Richard II.* v. 5, 94.

Line 588. *Jolthead*, blockhead, dunce. See *Two Gentlemen of Verona*, iii. 1, 290,—" Fie on thee, jolt-head! Thou canst not read." Also *Taming of the Shrew*, iv. 1, 169.

Line 590. *Rooke*=cheat or sharper, and is used as a general term of contempt. See *Every Man in his Humour*, i. 5, 89,— " Hang him, rook!" The host of the Garter frequently addresses his familiars as " bully-rook." See *Merry Wives of Windsor*, i. 3, 2 ; ii. 1, 200, 207, 213.

Line 611. *Forfeiture.*—Properly, something lost on engagement, or in consequence of the breach of an obligation. Cf. *Merchant of Venice*, i. 3, 165 ; iv. 1, 24, 122. Here the word is used in a modified and more general sense.

Line 641. *Ast.*—Cf., in 1592, G. Harvey's *Pierces Superer*, 57,—"He . . . bourdeth, girdeth, asseth, the excellentest writers."

Line 644. *Scindifer.*—So MS., possibly for *scimitar*.

Line 649. *Whineard*, a sword or hanger (Halliwell) :—

" His cloake grew large and sid
And a faire whinniard by his side."
(*Cobler of Canterburie*, 1608, sig. E, ii.)

Line 658. *Stingian.*—So MS. for *Stygian*.

Line 668. *Lovd.*—So MS., possibly for *livd*.

Line 670. *Vild.*—So MS. for *vile* or *wild*.

Lines 677, 678. *Christall* and *cherrye* reversed.

Line 683. *Headye*, rash, impetuous. See 1 *Henry IV.* ii. 3, 58, and *Henry V.* i. 1, 34.

Line 686. *Dicker.*—Ten of any commodity, as ten hides of leather, ten bars of iron, etc. This word comes from the late Latin *dicra* (*dicora, decora, dacra, dacrum*), classical Latin *decuria*, meaning ten hides, occasionally ten of other things. " Also that no maner foreyn sille no lether in the seid cite, but it be in the yelde halle of the same, paying for the custom of every *dyker* i.d." (*English Guilds*, ed. by Toulmin Smith, p. 384). For the wide use of the word in Western and Northern Europe, cf. O. Norse *dekr*, ten hides, M. H. G. *decker*, ten of anything, especially hides. Modern German *decker*=ten hides.

Line 688. *How* here = however, as in *Venus and Adonis*, 79 ; 1 *Henry IV.* v. 2, 12 ; and *Much Ado about Nothing*, iii. 1, 60.

Line 703. *Seas.*—MS. has *sea.*

Line 711. *Pinke.*—A word found in the northern dialects for
" to peep slyly." Cf. the adjective *pink,* winking, half-shut ;
" Plumpy Bacchus with pink eyne " (*Antony and Cleopatra,* ii.
7, 121).

Line 734. *My grandam . . . earth.*—Cf. 1 *Henry IV.* iii. 1, 34.

Line 735. *Randome.*—The verb random, to stray wildly, is
more frequently found with the original spelling *randon* (French
randoner, to run rapidly), which became altered, possibly by
analogy with *whilom* and *seldom,* possibly by a process of
change similar to that which converted *ranson* to *ransom.* Sack-
ville writes :—" Shall leave them free to randon of their will."

NOTES TO THE APPENDIX.

I.

Line 32. (*i*) is here equivalent to *id est.* Lilly gives the
examples of lines 52, 53 (in which the same abbreviation here
occurs) with the words written in full.

Line 48. *Repente.*—A play on the meaning of the English and
the form of the Latin word *repente* is clearly intended.

Line 70. " Denarii dicti, quod denos æris valebant ; quinarii,
quod quinos " (Varro).

Line 93. *Janus* is frequently, though not invariably, represented
in mythology as guardian of the entrance to heaven ; in which
capacity he holds in his right hand a staff, and in his left a key,
symbolical of his office (Ovid, *Fast.* i. 125). The names of
Jupiter and Janus were usually coupled in prayer, as the
divinities whose aid it was necessary to invoke at the beginning
of any undertaking. Jupiter gave by augury the requisite sanc-
tion ; but it was the part of Janus to confer a blessing at the
outset.

Line 111. *Hippocrise.*—A beverage composed of wine, with
spices and sugar, strained through a cloth ; said to have been
named from Hippocrates' sleeve, the term given by apothecaries
to a strainer (Halliwell).

Line 111. *Muskadine.*— A well-known rich wine.

"And I will have also wyne de Ryne
With new maid clarye, that is good and fyne,
Muscadell, terantyne, and bastard,
With Ypocras and Pyment comyng afterwarde."

(*MS. Rawl.* C. 86.)

Though *muscadell* is the usual form (for instances see Furnivall, *The Babees Book*, p. 205), the spelling *muscadine* occurs in Beaumont and Fletcher's *Loyal Subject*, iii. 4.

Line 112. *The Pierides pies.*—The reference is not to the Muses themselves (sometimes called Pierides from Pieria, near Olympus), but to the nine daughters of Pierus, who for attempting to rival the Muses were changed into birds of the magpie kind. For a full account of the transformation see Ovid, *Met.* v. 670, etc. There is a play here on the double meaning of *pie*, namely a bird (Latin pica), and an article of food.

II.

Line 23.—*Keele*, to cool; from O. E. célan, M. E. kelen. See *Love's Labour's Lost*, v. 2, 930—"While greasy Joan doth keel the pot." Usually, however, the verb bore the derived sense of "to keep from boiling over by stirring round." *A Tour to the Caves*, 1781, gives—"*Keel*, to keep the pot from boiling over." This is evidently the meaning which should be adopted here.

III.

Line 13. *It is bootles*, etc.—Puns on the different meanings of the word *boot* are very common in Elizabethan writers, and the relevant use of the one frequently entails the irrelevant introduction of the other. See, for example, *Two Gentlemen of Verona*, i. 1, 27, etc. :

"*Pro.* Over the boots ? Nay, give me not the boots.
Val. No, I will not, for it boots thee not."

And *Every Man in his Humour*, i. 3, 30, etc. :

"*Brai.* Why, you may ha' my master's gelding, to save your longing, sir.
Step. But I ha' no boots, that's the spite on't.
Brai. Why, a fine wisp of hay roll'd hard, Master Stephen.
Step. No, faith, it's no boot to follow him now."

" Give me not the boots" = "do not make a laughing-stock of me."

Line 48. *Ioynd stooles.*—The word joint-stool, meaning a seat made with joints, a folding-chair, is sometimes spelt *join'd stool* in old editions of Shakespeare. The porter's use of this form is probably intended to convey a jest ; *ioynd stooles* is here equivalent to stooles joined to one another, and the term is used as a facetious synonym for *bench.*

IV.

Line 6. *Oulde.*—So MS., possibly for *whole.*

Line 19. *A man & noe beast.*—An inversion, probably intentional.

Line 22. *Condole my tragedies.*—*Condole* is here used in the now obsolete transitive sense, and is equivalent to bewail, grieve over, lament. See (in 1607) Hieron, *Works*, i. 179—"How tender-hearted the Lord is, and how he doth . . . condole our miseries." Cf. also Pistol's use of the verb, *Henry V.* ii. 1, 133.

Line 24. *Craues.*—The substantive crave, = craving, is not in general use, but appears to be considered rather as a new formation than as an obsolete word. Thus the earliest of the three examples given in the N. E. D. dates from 1830—"His crave and his vanity so far deluded him" (*Fraser's Magazine*, i. 134). This is a clear instance of a previous use.

The sentence as it stands presents some difficulty, inasmuch as the porter has made in the course of his speech only two distinct petitions, namely that he may be forgiven "all delictes and crimes" (l. 10), and that his black staff may be restored to him (l. 18). Perhaps the delicate hint concerning "my ladye pecunia," coupled with the appeal to "the profunditye or abisse" of the President's liberality, is to be considered as constituting a third.